D1547068

Blaze Erupting

Also from Rebecca Zanetti

SCORPIUS SYNDROME SERIES
Scorpius Rising
Mercury Striking
Shadow Falling
Justice Ascending
Storm Gathering

DARK PROTECTORS
Fated
Claimed
Tempted
Hunted
Consumed
Provoked
Twisted
Shadowed
Tamed
Marked
Teased
Tricked
Tangled
Talen

REALM ENFORCERS
Wicked Ride
Wicked Edge
Wicked Burn
Wicked Kiss
Wicked Bite

SIN BROTHERS
Forgotten Sins
Sweet Revenge
Blind Faith
Total Surrender

BLOOD BROTHERS
Deadly Silence
Lethal Lies
Twisted Truths

MAVERICK MONTANA
Against the Wall
Under the Covers
Rising Assets
Over the Top

Blaze Erupting

Scorpius Syndrome/A Brigade Novella

By Rebecca Zanetti

1001 Dark Nights

EVIL EYE
CONCEPTS

BLAZE ERUPTING: Scorpius Syndrome/A Brigade Novella
By Rebecca Zanetti

Copyright 2018 Rebecca Zanetti
ISBN: 978-1-948050-07-4

Foreword: Copyright 2014 M. J. Rose

Published by Evil Eye Concepts, Incorporated

Dedication

This one is for MJ Rose, who'd be a well-organized leader if the apocalypse really did come to pass. Thank you for your vision and for all that you do.

Acknowledgments from the Author

Thank you to Elizabeth Berry and MJ Rose for bringing together this wonderful group of authors and friends. The combination of your vision, your hard work, and your dedication is an inspiration to us all.

Thank you to Jillian Stein, who is not only a phenomenal social media guru but a wonderful friend.

Steve Berry, thank you for your generosity with sharing your insights and experience in the book industry.

Thank you to Kimberly Guidroz, Fedora Chen, and Kasi Alexander for their dedication and awesome insights.

Thanks also to Asha Hossain, who creates absolutely fantastic book covers.

As always, a lot of love and a huge thank you goes to Big Tone, Gabe and Karly, my amazing family who is so supportive.

Finally, thank you to Rebecca's Rebels, my street team, who have been so generous with their time and friendship. Thank you to Minga Portillo for her excellent leadership of the team. And last, but not least, thank you to all of my readers who spend time with my characters.

~ RAZ

Sign up for the 1001 Dark Nights Newsletter
and be entered to win a Tiffany Key necklace.

There's a contest every month!

Go to www.1001DarkNights.com to subscribe.

As a bonus, all subscribers will receive a free copy of
Discovery Bundle Three
Featuring stories by
Sidney Bristol, Darcy Burke, T. Gephart
Stacey Kennedy, Adrian Locke
JB Salsbury, and Erika Wilde

One Thousand and One Dark Nights

Once upon a time, in the future…

*I was a student fascinated with stories and learning.
I studied philosophy, poetry, history, the occult, and
the art and science of love and magic. I had a vast
library at my father's home and collected thousands
of volumes of fantastic tales.*

*I learned all about ancient races and bygone
times. About myths and legends and dreams of all
people through the millennium. And the more I read
the stronger my imagination grew until I discovered
that I was able to travel into the stories… to actually
become part of them.*

*I wish I could say that I listened to my teacher
and respected my gift, as I ought to have. If I had, I
would not be telling you this tale now.
But I was foolhardy and confused, showing off
with bravery.*

*One afternoon, curious about the myth of the
Arabian Nights, I traveled back to ancient Persia to
see for myself if it was true that every day Shahryar
(Persian: شهريار, "king") married a new virgin, and then
sent yesterday's wife to be beheaded. It was written
and I had read, that by the time he met Scheherazade,
the vizier's daughter, he'd killed one thousand
women.*

Something went wrong with my efforts. I arrived in the midst of the story and somehow exchanged places with Scheherazade – a phenomena that had never occurred before and that still to this day, I cannot explain.

Now I am trapped in that ancient past. I have taken on Scheherazade's life and the only way I can protect myself and stay alive is to do what she did to protect herself and stay alive.

Every night the King calls for me and listens as I spin tales. And when the evening ends and dawn breaks, I stop at a point that leaves him breathless and yearning for more. And so the King spares my life for one more day, so that he might hear the rest of my dark tale.

As soon as I finish a story... I begin a new one... like the one that you, dear reader, have before you now.

Chapter One

I convinced my boss that Hugh is the guy to help us. I think he is. But it's possible... I just want to see him again.
—Dr. Eleanor Smithers, Brigade Notes

Hugh Johnson knew within a second of entering his bungalow that somebody else was inside. First, his hound dog didn't bother to meet him at the door. Second, a vaguely familiar scent of wild bluebells wafted in the air.

He tossed his keys near the bowl sitting on an entryway table his mama had insisted he own and kept walking down the hallway, striding into his comfortable living room with its floor-to-ceiling windows that showcased trees and a bubbling brook outside. There he stopped cold. "Ellie," he murmured, his normally relaxed body going on full alert as he took in the small woman lounging on his worn couch with the dog's head in her lap.

She smiled pretty pink lips, her blue eyes sparkling behind wire-rimmed glasses as she stroked the dog's head. "Your door was unlocked."

Heisenberg groaned happily beneath her palm, keeping his eyes closed in pure bliss.

Hugh had the oddest desire to change places with the dog. "Not much crime out here in eastern Kentucky," he murmured, studying the woman he hadn't seen in...what? Ten years? "You're all grown up, Eleanor."

"I should hope so." Even though she was wearing a black pencil skirt and fancy silk shirt, she'd kicked her shoes off and had her legs, her long and bare legs, on the hunting and fishing magazines scattered across his coffee table. She'd shoved a tattered and well-read Steve Berry thriller to the side.

Her ankles were crossed, and her toenails were painted with purple sparkles. Her blonde hair reached her shoulders in the wild mass he remembered. "You're looking...good," she murmured, a slight pink filling her cheeks.

He'd always liked how easily she blushed. Then he glanced down at his ripped jeans and threadbare Metallica T-shirt. "I'm on vacation."

"It's over," she said softly, her gaze sobering.

His heartrate ticked slightly. Not much, but some. He scratched behind his ear and then stuck his thumbs in his jeans pockets. "It's great to see you and all, but what are you doing here?" He hadn't seen her since they'd both graduated with their bachelor degrees in chemistry from Kentucky.

"That's it?" She tilted her head to the side in a way he remembered as being cute. Now, on her all grown up, it was sexy. Very. "No Southern hospitality? No...have a beer?"

All right. He'd never been much of a game player, but he was on vacation from his job after a pain-in-the-ass month, and a beer sounded fucking fantastic. Not much threw him off balance, and right now, he wasn't liking the feeling in his gut. So he moved for the kitchen, leaned down to open the short and round fridge, and drew out two bottles. A quick flip of the tops, and he strode for her, handing over the ultra-cold brew. "If I remember right, you don't like beer," he murmured before lifting his bottle and taking a big swig.

She eyed him over hers and took a delicate drink. "I'm surprised you remember me at all."

His eyebrows lifted of their own accord. "You were my lab partner for two years. We were friends. Why wouldn't I remember you?" Not once had he ever truly understood what was in the woman's head.

She lifted a small shoulder, her gaze even and veiled. Interesting. That was a skill she'd acquired after college, apparently. "You were always surrounded by girls. Figured I was one of many."

He sat in the chair adjacent to the couch and kicked a pair of boots out of his way. "I was the quarterback on the football team." Which had led to a bunch of dates. "Until I wasn't." The day he'd blown his knee out in his senior year had changed the life he had planned. One hit and it was over. Completely. He grinned. "We never slept together, Ell. That made you one of...one." It was true, and they both knew it.

She snorted, her nose pert and scattered with freckles. "You were definitely a man-whore."

He thoughtfully took another drink. She was pretty. Very. Small hips, little waist, high breasts. His body came alive in a way it hadn't in a surprisingly long time. "Come here to scratch an itch that never quite went away?"

Her jaw dropped and then snapped shut. "Of course not, you egomaniac." More pink in her cheeks.

"Sorry." The words came out before he could think. "There was a time, after my injury, when I'm pretty sure I was a complete ass." The three months after, when the football scouts stopped calling were a blur, but he could remember her bringing him...what? Cookies? And his homework. Yeah. That, he remembered. "If I did anything that irritated you, I'm very sorry, Eleanor." He meant every damn word. Without her, he probably wouldn't have graduated.

She took another drink. "You were cranky. Like a bear with a thorn in its paw. But you weren't mean, Hugh." She sighed. "I don't think you have that in you."

The woman was wrong. Everybody had that in them. Now more than ever. Memories started flooding back. Working with Ellie. Her smile and her sense of humor...and her way of carefully thinking everything through before saying anything. Oh, she'd get to her reason for being in his place, but she'd do it in her time. He could live with that. "Where have you been, anyway?"

She glanced down at the dog, who was almost purring in her lap. "Here and there. Graduate school. Chemistry and computer science," she answered before he could ask.

He grinned. "Dr. Smithers. It fits you." Then he paused, surprised by how unsettling his next thought was. "If that's still your name. Did you get married?" Why did the thought feel like a punch to the nards? He hadn't seen her in eons.

"No." She wetted her lips.

His pants tightened. "Me either."

"I know," she said softly, meeting his gaze again. "I have a dossier on you."

A dossier? What the fuck? "All right." He set his beer on the table and leaned forward. "Enough easing in, Ellie. What the hell are you doing here?"

She sighed and dropped her feet to the shag carpet, careful not to dislodge the dog. Her shoulders straightened and she lowered her chin in a stubborn motion that wasn't familiar. "Congratulations. You've been transferred from the Domestic Nuclear Detection Office, Hugh."

Transferred? He straightened. "Sorry, but I like my job and my life." It was quiet, methodical, and routine.

"That's too bad. Because now you work for the Brigade." She smiled while her eyes remained deadly serious. "Welcome to the first line of defense against any current pandemic Scorpius-induced threats."

* * * *

Ellie let her words sink in and tried not to stare at the man who still ran through her dreams periodically. It wasn't fair. It really wasn't.

Couldn't he have a slight paunch? Or a receding hairline? Or adult acne?

No. Hugh Johnson had gone from an adorable college kid to a ripped and sexy man. The guy looked like a dark Thor with his thick brown hair and angled jaw, obvious even when covered with a two-day scruff. His eyes, those deep ocean-blue eyes, were still sharp and sexy. Oh, he moved like a good old Southern boy, slow and graceful, but anybody with eyes could see the intelligence in his. Most people didn't bother to look.

She always had.

When she hadn't been dreaming of him sweeping her up and declaring undying love. Man, she'd been a moron.

"I'm not leaving my job, Ellie," he said, his voice a deep rumble with a gentle tone.

That voice. Man, she remembered it. Her abdomen clenched, and tingles danced down her spine. "They sent me in to ease your way," she explained, only lying a little bit. Okay. She might have volunteered, but still. The plan was good. "The DNDO is part of Homeland Security, which means you can be transferred. You have been. Get on board."

One of his dark eyebrows rose. "You've gotten a bit bossy, sweetheart."

He had no idea. She breathed out. "Listen, Hugh. The pandemic is killing people left and right." The Scorpius bacteria had already killed a hundred thousand people, and it showed no chance of slowing down. "The world is dying, and we're under a threat."

"I'm not a biologist, and you know it. The CDC will find a cure," he countered, not sounding sure.

"I hope so." She glanced at the full trees outside. "But that's their job. Ours is to protect the country in the meantime."

He frowned. "I'm not agreeing, but what's the Brigade?"

She straightened. "It's a small force appointed by the president to counter the difficulties we're about to have, and we need your help. Your expertise as the assistant director of assessments for DNDO."

He leaned back. "I'm third in line, Ellie. I like it that way. You need the director or the deputy director."

Actually, the man was twice as smart as the other two. "We want you."

The words hung in the air. He studied her, looking suddenly...hungry.

She swallowed, her lungs compressing. "We can guarantee the safety of your family. There are places being set up—places the Scorpius bacterium shouldn't touch."

He shook his head, the movement measured. "Scorpius is going to touch everywhere, and you should know that." He finished his beer, his tough-guy neck moving as he swallowed. Then he set the bottle down. "My family has all headed for the hills. We have cabins around Blue Lake, and my folks and brothers are hunkering down."

She tilted her head. "Yet you stayed here." Ah. The man wasn't as oblivious as he appeared. "You knew you'd be needed."

His chin lowered. "I've made assessments regarding nuclear threats for the last five years. Yeah, baby. I knew I'd be needed."

Tingles exploded along her skin. It was nice when he dropped the good-ole-boy act. Even though it was only partly an act. "Did your dad fight you on closing the tire stores?" She remembered his family had owned several tire stores throughout the South and both of his brothers had gone to work there. Not him. He'd wanted something different. Money be damned.

"No."

Good. His family had seemed like nice people. "I'm glad," she murmured.

"What about your mom? How is she?" Hugh asked.

So he remembered a little about her. Even so, her smile felt sad. "She died a few years back. Breast cancer." Ellie's only family.

"I'm so sorry."

"Me too." She cleared her throat and gently moved the snoring mutt off her lap, slipping her feet into her pumps. "I assume you have a go-bag ready?"

"No." He glared at the dog. "Get off the couch, Heisenberg."

Ellie stood, hiding a smile when the pooch totally ignored his master. "Cute name." She looked around. "You're also welcome to bring a significant other with you. If you have one."

He stood and towered over her so suddenly she stopped breathing. "Are you asking me if I'm available, Ellie Mae?"

Warmth from his body, his very *close* body, washed over her. She tilted her head back to meet his eyes. "Don't call me that." It was his little nickname for her in college, and her heart used to stutter every time he used it. Something special just between the two of them.

"Why not?" He stepped in until their feet touched.

She blinked. Sparks flew between her nerves. "Wh-what are you doing?"

"Exploring." His gaze ran over her face, curiosity clearly gleaming in those deep eyes. "I liked you. Back then. Big eyes, sweet smile, huge brain." He reached out and brushed a curl away from her cheek, his touch warm.

Her throat closed. Heat flashed from his touch, down her torso, to zing along her erogenous zones. "Yet the one time I made a move, you rejected me." It still hurt. When he was down and out—injured and in pain—she'd tried to give comfort.

"I wasn't lookin' for forever, and you're a forever type of gal," he murmured, standing way too close. "That offer you made nearly killed me sayin' no. But even though I was hurtin' and wanted to stop the pain, I couldn't hurt you. Ever." As if he couldn't help himself, he brushed his knuckles along her jawline. "But I wanted you, Ell. Just knew you'd be a mistake I'd never recover from."

Her lungs released quickly, and she took a step sideways along the coffee table. "Agreed."

Amusement tilted his lips. "I ain't a college kid no more, Ellie."

"I'm well aware of that." She needed to go by him to get to the door, and he wasn't moving out of the way. How in the world did he still affect her like this? It had been years, for goodness' sake. "We're both eons out of college."

"I'm no longer hurtin' or whorin' around," he continued, looking big and broad in the small room.

"Your point?" she snapped, trying to get her libido under some semblance of control. Why did his country-boy act turn her on? She needed a shrink. Bad.

"My point? Well now." His smile was more wolf than sheepdog. "This time, when you make the offer? I'm gonna say yes."

Chapter Two

Day 1. I don't write in a diary, and this is stupid but is apparently part of the job. The Brigade is an odd group. There. That should do it for the day.
—Hugh Johnson, Brigade Notes

Hugh stepped out of the chauffeured vehicle and reached a hand in to assist Ellie after a two-hour flight to Springfield. Litter tumbled down the cracked sidewalk, mixing with dried leaves. "Somebody had better explain what is going on," he said, shutting the vehicle door, not surprised when it zoomed down the quiet street and away from them. They'd reminisced about college for the entire plane ride because she wouldn't answer any of his questions during the trip.

"I told you I'm not authorized to detail mission parameters to you." Ellie turned and looked down the deserted street. "You used to be more patient."

He glanced at the quiet stone building in front of them. A cool wind washed down the street located at the edge of the city complete with several abandoned buildings. "You've never kidnapped me and brought me to Missouri before." This was all getting weird. Really weird. Rumor had it that Scorpius survivors, some of them, went completely serial-killer nuts. He glanced down at the petite woman to his right.

She snorted. "I'm not planning on caging you, buddy." Setting her shoulders, she marched on fairly high heels up the crumbling steps to push open the front door.

He kicked himself into gear and rushed after her, holding the door for her to enter. She had to brush by him, and his skin sensitized.

Why had he let her out of his sight so long ago?

Shaking himself out of the past, he grasped her arm and pulled her to a halt. Scratched and thin oak made up the floor, and dingy paint covered the walls. Several real wooden doors, old and dented, took up residence every few yards, proclaiming businesses. Henry O'Toole, attorney at law. Mildren Kremis, accountant. And so on. "Where the hell are we?" he asked.

She sighed and tugged him over to an old-fashioned elevator. "Just get in."

The thing wobbled from his weight as he stepped inside. "Um—" he muttered as the door closed.

She pressed the button for the second floor, then the first, then the third, second, first, second, and then the close-door button.

Good God. She'd lost her mind. "Have you survived Scorpius?" he asked, keeping his tone mild. He'd just crossed states with a crazy woman.

Her smile touched something in him. "Hold on, Ace." Then she pressed the red alarm button.

The elevator dropped suddenly, and he grabbed the wall. "Ellie?" His breath quickened.

She chuckled. They descended rapidly and then...stopped. The door opened.

He moved before she could, instinctively protecting her and stepping out, keeping her behind him. Two armed marines stood guard in front of what looked like a steel door set into a steel wall. His shoulders relaxed. "This is interesting."

Ellie shoved past him and handed her ID to the guy on the left. "Used to be a CIA compound." The guard returned her credentials and opened the steel door.

In Missouri? He gave the soldiers a nod and then followed her down another long hallway that led to a round control room with screens on every wall. Several people worked away at consoles, not bothering to look up at them. He whistled. "Impressive."

"This way." She led him around the consoles to a smaller control room with a long conference room type table.

He walked inside and paused.

Two people, a man and a woman, sat at the table eating what looked like burgers. They wore casual jeans, boots, and T-shirts. The man stood, all six-foot-four of him, and held out a hand. He had dark brown hair, intense green eyes, and a scar down his neck. "Hugh. Thanks for coming." The Scottish brogue was a surprise.

Hugh shook his hand. "Somebody had better start explaining."

The woman stood to about five-foot-seven, with dark eyes and curly brown hair. She also held out a hand. "I'm Nora Medina, and this is Deacan McDougall. Welcome to the Brigade." Her voice was cultured and her eyes spirited. She gestured to the other side of the table and retook her seat.

"McDougall," Deacan said easily, pulling fries out of a bag. "Nora McDougall."

Nora blinked and then nodded. "That's right. I'd forgotten."

McDougall eyed his wife. "Apparently, I'll have to remind you later."

Ellie sighed. "Newlyweds," she whispered to Hugh. "Please. Have a seat."

Hugh cut Ellie a look and crossed around to sit.

McDougall shoved a greasy-looking bag toward him and retook his seat. "Can't vouch for the cholesterol content, but the burgers are excellent."

Hugh nudged the bag toward Ellie. "I'm here for one more minute if somebody doesn't explain." While he kept his voice level, the hair was rising on the back of his neck. He was a simple guy, and this espionage bullshit just pissed him off. "Fifty seconds."

McDougall grinned. "I have two armed marines guarding the elevator. Think you can go through both of them?"

"If I have to," Hugh said easily. He might not be in the military, but he'd learned how to fight at a young age. With two brothers, it was impossible not to know how to take and throw a punch. He missed them already. At least Milo had promised to fetch the dog and take him to the lake. Heisenberg loved chasing the gulls. "I guess I could start with you."

McDougall's smile widened. The guy wasn't put off in the slightest. "I like you already, Johnson."

Wonderful. "Being liked has never been one of my goals," Hugh said smoothly. Except by Ellie. At the moment, he'd freakin' love it if she liked him. Especially enough to get naked. It had been way too long.

"Gentlemen," Nora said in the way women had been sighing the words through history—like all men were morons. "Let's get down to business." She drew a remote control out from under the table and pointed it at the screen on the far wall. "We've downloaded your records from work, Hugh." His computer screen took shape.

He sat back. "Did you, now?" he asked mildly, his ears starting to itch.

"Eleanor did," Nora said absently, clicking a file open.

He slowly turned his head to face the blushing blonde. "You hacked my system, Ellie?"

* * * *

Ellie barely kept from fidgeting in her chair when faced with Hugh's calm stare. Anybody who didn't know him would think he was mildly curious. But she did know him—better than she'd thought. His eyes burned a deep blue. The guy was pissed. "We thought it expedient to have your records here for you," she said, sounding like a prim schoolmarm with a stick up her butt. She held back a wince. "You're welcome."

His gaze remained on her face for a few heated beats. "You work for the government as a computer scientist?"

Deke snorted. "That's the understatement of the year."

Hugh turned toward Deke. "Ten seconds."

Deke snatched a couple of Nora's fries before she could stop him. "The president has sanctioned the Brigade as a line of defense against problems caused by the Scorpius Pandemic. We're the Brigade. As you know, the government has been concerned for years about a terrorist attack against a nuclear facility."

Hugh's broad chest visibly settled. "You have intel?"

"We have chatter. A lot of it," Ellie said quietly. "It's unclear and garbled, but based on information from several sources, we believe there is going to be an attack soon."

"Terrorists are taking advantage of the pandemic. That makes a sick kind of sense. Where?" Hugh asked.

Deke sighed. "We're hoping you can tell us where. Not only the best three targets but the most probable terrorists. Think on US soil—either visiting here or homegrown. Commercial air traffic has been shut down. Probably for a long time."

"Probably for good if nobody gets a handle on the Scorpius bacteria," Ellie murmured, feeling better with Hugh at her side.

Hugh eyed McDougall.

Deke nodded. "I'm military and always have been. The president, who's currently fighting the illness, tapped me for the Brigade. Nora is a microbiologist, and Eleanor is a computer scientist. You'll meet the rest of the team later."

Hugh turned toward Nora. "Microbiologist? Shouldn't you be in a lab right now fixing this thing?"

Her dark eyes twinkled. "My best friend is the head of infectious diseases at the CDC. Her name is Lynne Harmony, and she's fighting this thing even though she's been infected. If she needs me, she'll call. I'm needed here."

"Lynne Harmony? The woman whose heart was turned blue by a faulty cure? I'd heard she'd died," Hugh said quietly.

"No. She's alternating between being a test subject and working as a doctor," Nora said, losing her smile. "If anybody can find a cure for this bug, it's Lynne. For now, we have other threats."

"What is our biggest threat nuclear-wise?" Deke asked, somber now.

Hugh breathed out, his jaw looking hard. "Depends on several factors. First, look for older facilities with outdated security coupled with the biggest casualty possibility. Second, look at where Scorpius has hit hardest...because those places will have lightened security. Third, look at locations of known or suspected terrorist organizations on our soil."

Nausea rolled in Ellie's stomach. Her hand itched with the urge to take Hugh's. To feel his strength and warmth. To find comfort. So she clasped both hands in her lap. She was an adult with an important job, and she needed to buck up and stop this nonsense.

Deke pushed away from the table. "Good. You and Eleanor have an hour to create a list of likely targets and suspects. We'll cross-reference your list with our counter-terrorism expert's list. Hopefully there will be a common denominator."

Nora gracefully stood and crossed around the table. "We should be back in an hour or so."

Deke nodded and waited until she'd reached him. "I'm going to check in with the president. Hopefully he'll be one of the survivors of this thing. Otherwise, Congressman Bret Atherton will step up as our new leader."

Ellie caught an odd tone. "You don't like Atherton?"

Deke shrugged a massive shoulder. "I don't know the guy, and at this point, knowledge is power. I like the current president. We'll also check in with Lynne Harmony and see what's going on with what's left of the CDC."

Nora bit her lip, amusement dancing in her dark eyes. "If you get finished early, Eleanor can show you the sleeping quarters, Hugh."

Was her friend matchmaking? Ellie gave her a look while trying to be casual. "I'd be happy to show Hugh around," she said.

Nora's lips visibly twitched.

Deke grasped her arm and drew her from the room. "You're terrible," he murmured loud enough to make Ellie blush.

The room quieted and somehow electrified.

"You've been working with Homeland?" Hugh asked, no expression on his hard face.

She swallowed. "Mostly. I started with the CIA and then moved over." So yes, they'd been working for the same agency for the last five years but in different divisions and locations.

"Did you know?" he asked softly, too softly.

She thought about lying. She really did. "I knew." Facing him, she forced a smile. "I kept track of you a little bit. Nothing stalkerish or anything. I always wanted the best for you." It was true. Even though he'd broken her heart when absolutely not meaning to do so, she'd wanted him to have a good life.

"Why didn't you reach out?" He did exactly that, his thumb and forefinger grasping her chin so she couldn't look away.

Why not? The one time she'd tried, he'd rejected her. Sure, he'd been hurt and angry and possibly had not wanted to use her, which made him decent. But still. "I've been busy," she said, a bit lamely if asked.

"You haven't married."

Was that satisfaction in his gaze?

She gently tugged her face free. "No, but I was engaged until a couple of months ago." So there.

His hand dropped to his lap. "Why did you call it off?"

Now that was sweet. She tried for flirty, narrowing her eyes. "Who said *I* called it off?"

He frowned. "Is there something in your eye?"

Crap. She blinked. "It's okay now. Um, I called it off because it just didn't feel right." Kyle was a good guy. A marine sniper. But something was missing, and even he seemed relieved when she said they should go on like friends. "He's a great guy. Stationed overseas for now." Why was she always in the friend zone with great guys? Wasn't this the time of the geek?

Hugh reached for the remote control, rolling slightly away from her. "I guess we should get to work."

Relief flushed down her. She was so much better at work than at feelings. "Yes." Opening a cabinet behind her chair, she drew out several notepads, pens, and highlighters. Then she set them carefully on the table, back in control of herself.

"I'm glad we didn't date in college," Hugh said absently, opening several more file folders on the screen.

Hurt slid through her, and she calmed her expression. "Really? Why?"

He paused, turning to face her, his eyes burning. "Because we have nothing bad from the past to deal with." He smiled, the sight a bit intimidating. "It's a new start for us."

Chapter Three

The end of the world has most likely started. But I have Nora by my side, so we'll create a better world. Hopefully.
—Deacan Devlin McDougall, Brigade Notes

Deke finished checking the armory, pleased with the organization set into place by Connor Lewis, the guy in charge of weapons. A whisper of sound caught his attention, and he turned to see Nora by the door. "Sweetheart?"

She leaned against the doorframe, looking luscious in her tight jeans and blue shirt. "There's a credible threat against the Internet. A virus that can infect the servers."

Shit. He slipped a Glock into its slot and turned completely to face her, his mind rapidly calculating variables. "I'll contact a friend in the Teams. We have to take out the nuclear threat." More people were in danger from that. Well, probably. "Then we'll go after the hackers."

She nodded, her stunning eyes somber. "What do you think of him? Of Hugh?"

Deke studied the woman who held his heart and always would. "You're more insightful than I am. What do you think?"

She bit her lip, making him want to take a bite as well. "I like him. The country-boy act is both genuine and fun, but he's obviously bright. And he didn't balk at jumping into the fray here with us."

Deke scratched the scruff at his jaw. He'd forgotten to shave again. "Ivan's analysis seemed spot on, while I'd have to say that Eleanor's was a little nostalgic." He'd just put together his team, and he was still learning their tics. Eleanor's weak spot seemed to be Hugh Johnson himself. "I do like the guy, though I don't want my computer specialist distracted."

Nora moved for him then, sliding her hands up his bare arms. His body sprang to life. "Why not? Distraction is good."

He had to agree with her there. Except when he lowered his head to take her mouth, movement at the door stopped him. Damn it. He paused, looking up to see his intelligence specialist waiting expectantly. "Ivan?"

Ivan Milleroff was so smart he was dangerous. Deke had scouted the genius from the CIA the second he'd put together the Brigade, and even he didn't know what all was in Ivan's personnel file. Ivan cocked his head to the side, his eyes burning. "The president is dead. Bret Atherton is stepping up within the hour."

Deke straightened, his chest filling. He'd liked the president. Both of the now deceased presidents, actually. "Things are changing too fast."

"Amen to that," Ivan said. He paused. "And there might be a problem with your boy. With Hugh. Just found it."

Ah, shit.

* * * *

Hugh finished gathering his notes just as the rest of the Brigade filed into the conference room for introductions.

"Hugh? Meet Ivan Milleroff, who's our intelligence specialist," Deke said, pulling out a chair at the head of the table.

Ivan had dark eyes, short brown hair, and a veiled stare. If one wasn't looking closely, his eyes would appear blank. They weren't. He was tall and lean, every movement economical. There was no doubt the guy was a threat. A serious one. They shook hands.

Another man, this one a black man well over six feet tall, strode into the room. He wore jeans and a leather jacket with a gun strapped to his thigh and a knife to his calf. "I'm Connor Lewis." His voice was deep and rich, and his handshake firm.

Hugh released him and settled back in his seat. Tension rolled through the small space. What was happening? "What do you do around here?"

"I bury the bodies," Connor said easily, pulling out a chair. "Better hope you're not one of them."

Ah. Alrighty then. Hugh watched Ellie out of the corner of his eye. She appeared calm and unflappable as she straightened her papers into a neat stack. "Have all of you worked together long?" he asked.

"Some," Deke said as the rest of the gang secured chairs. "Different jobs, different locations. Nothing as important as right here and right now." His Scottish brogue remained just under the surface, a hint of the complexity of the leader. "We do have a question for you, Hugh."

Yeah. He'd kind of gotten that feeling. "Hey. You asked me to the dance here." It wasn't like he'd wanted to leave his vacation. Whatever the tension was in the room was starting to tick him off.

Ellie leaned forward. "What's happening?"

Deke took the remote control and pointed it at the screen, bringing up a very familiar face. "This is Gregor Valentino, who's a known gun runner with ties to several terrorist organizations. And this—" he clicked again and brought up a picture of Hugh meeting with Gregor "—is you."

Hugh leaned back. "Impressive. Where did you find that?" Who the hell had managed to take that picture?

"FBI buddy," Deke said easily, taking out a Glock to place on the table.

"Hey—" Ellie said, rolling her chair toward Hugh.

Toward him. That one movement dug right past his irritation and planted in his heart. He wanted to mess with McDougall a little, but Ellie had gone pale. Oh well. He knew how to do his job. "I don't know that guy. However, a picture like that showed up at my office with a demand for money. A lot of it."

Deke studied him. "You're saying somebody doctored this picture and then tried to blackmail you?"

"Yep," Hugh lied. "Took it to my boss, and they opened a file and contacted the FBI to create a case. Tried to track the guy down but no luck so far." He smiled. "That's all I can tell you." Which was the absolute truth.

Deke nodded at Ellie. "If you're telling the truth, she'll be able to discover that with her handy old computer."

If she was that good, she was damn impressive. Hugh shot her a smile. "Go for it."

She glanced at Deke and then drew her laptop out of her bag, quickly typing. "Whoa," she breathed. "I have top clearance all of a sudden. I mean, the top of the top." Her eyes sparkled. "I didn't even have to hack." Her lips turned down.

Hugh barely kept from barking out a laugh. The woman was disappointed that she didn't get to hack?

Ellie breathed out. "I'm running into roadblocks about this Gregor person." Then she frowned again. "The records containing your report haven't been added to the server yet. They must still be on your supervisor's computer."

"Wonderful," Hugh said. Deep cover meant deep cover, damn it. "If you're that good of a hacker, you should be able to get in there, right?"

Ellie read her screen. "Maybe. I need to go to the FBI if they have this picture."

Deke blew out air. "Fine. I'll make a call, and if anybody is still staffing at the FBI, we should have the files by tonight."

It was beyond sweet that she believed him so easily, even when he wasn't telling the truth. Hugh's chest hurt, and he thought briefly about breaking cover. But he'd taken an oath. "I'm telling the truth."

Ellie stared at Deke. "Even if you don't trust him yet, I'm asking you to trust me. He's innocent."

Hugh tried not to blanch.

Deke's nostrils flared. "I do trust you, Dr. Smithers. But you have to find his report."

She nodded, looking back at her computer. "With our new clearance level, who knows what we could read? I wonder if there's information on Marilyn Monroe in here." Her voice quickened. "Or information on the royal family."

Hugh grinned. He'd forgotten how much she liked reading about the royal family. It was a cute oddity, and he'd thought so even back in college. "I guess some things never change," he mused quietly.

Her smile showed a very small dimple in her right cheek.

"Later," Deke said, sliding his gun back into place. Apparently, he figured somebody else could shoot Hugh if necessary. "We have more immediate concerns. What have you two found regarding nuclear threats?"

Hugh hadn't ever been much of a talker and saw no reason to start now. "Ellie?"

She looked up, her intelligent eyes focusing behind the glasses. "We used an algorithm to determine the greatest nuclear threats on our soil. Factors included vulnerability of facility, number of potential casualties, and proximity to a major Scorpius outbreak."

Connor leaned in. "Why proximity to outbreak?"

"Because resources will be stretched thin," Ellie said, her voice reminding Hugh of their college days when they'd discussed common ion effect and buffers. "People will be concentrating on staying healthy or healing ill family members. Security guards will be away from post— either infected or concerned with more personal matters. Mostly."

"That was the easier part," Hugh said, glancing at his papers. "Best three nuclear power plants to hit at the present moment are in New York, Pennsylvania, and Arizona."

"Great," Nora said, shoving thick hair away from her face. "So a terrorist could just attack a facility and let off a nuclear bomb?"

Hugh shook his head. "No. The fuel for uranium reactors isn't enriched enough to explode like a bomb. The concern is meltdown or attack, which would release radiation in copious amounts or theft of the materials. It wouldn't be the first time a terrorist group tried to get its hands on uranium to make a dirty bomb." The idea rolled bile through his stomach and up his throat.

Ellie nodded. "A group could also target spent fuel, which are the pools where nuclear waste is kept. They could plant bombs there."

Connor sighed. "What happens then?"

"Boom," Hugh said grimly. "It would cause a catastrophic fire that would be worse than any nuclear meltdown. The radiation would be swept up in the smoke, which would carry far and wide. It'd be a disaster of unimaginable proportions."

Ivan had kept quiet for the entire interchange. "You're the expert, Hugh. If you were going to attack, how and where would you do it?"

Hugh rubbed his chin. The guy got right to the point, didn't he? "Unless I had contacts in New York, I'd go for Arizona or Pennsylvania. I'd take out the computer system and bring down the cameras, which would have to be from the inside, and make sure the cooling system stopped working."

Ellie cleared her throat. "You'd need one of the best hackers in the world to do that. There are safeguards upon safeguards in place for coolants."

Hugh nodded. "Yeah. If I was going to attack a nuclear power plant, I'd have the best in the world in my pocket." His body started to ache and he released each muscle to try uselessly to rid himself of tension. "Then I'd plant explosives around the spent fuel."

"It's nice you've planned this out," Connor muttered.

Hugh flashed a grin, amusement filling him. They were truly suspicious of him. "It's my job. At least, it was my job." He had a feeling everything had just changed.

"Suspects?" Deke asked.

Ellie pressed a button, and faces started filling the wall screen. "We've narrowed it down to five organizations in the states. Two homegrown and three Hugh has been watching for a year. They have the skills and means."

"It's one of these?" Ivan asked, leaning forward.

Hugh ran through the data. "Maybe. We don't know who else has shown up the last month as we all concentrated on Scorpius and the outbreak. There could be players on our soil that I haven't tracked."

"Just great," Connor said, eyeing the screen. "What now?"

Ellie set her papers down. "We go to the sites and look for anything out of the ordinary. I can only get into the computers onsite and not remotely."

"Affirmative." Deke shoved away from the table. "As of right now, you all have top-level clearance. There's nothing you can't request or see." He assisted Nora from her chair. "I think you're right about New York. Resources have been sent to the bigger cities for protection, and it'd be too hard to hit."

Man, Hugh hoped he was right. "Or that's what they're expecting we'll think."

Deke nodded. "Aye. That. For now, we check out the other two plants. Nora, Ivan, and I will fly to Pennsylvania since private planes haven't been grounded yet. Ivan has expertise here as well. Eleanor, Hugh, and Connor? You guys fly to the Arizona plant. I'll ask the new president to grease the wheels for you."

Connor stood. "And if Hugh is a problem?"

"Shoot him," Deke said absently.

Hugh coughed. Wonderful. He was going to work with these people?

Connor moved for the door. "Everyone needs to be properly suited up. Satellite phone, weapons, and protective gear. I have everything ready in the armory."

Hugh kept his face blank. Protective gear? Something told him that didn't mean condoms.

Just what the hell had he gotten involved in?

Chapter Four

I have a job to do. Now isn't the time for romance. No matter how wide his chest or tight his butt.
—Dr. Eleanor Smithers, Brigade Notes that nobody will ever see

The nuclear power plant in Arizona consisted of multiple buildings, parking areas, and round structures releasing tons of what looked like steam into the very blue sky.

Ellie kept her gaze off Hugh as they waited for the security guard to finish checking their credentials. Okay. One peek.

Yeah. He looked like a badass with a gun strapped to his thigh and a Homeland Security jacket covering a bulletproof vest which spanned a very broad chest. Even more intriguing, he appeared perfectly comfortable with both.

The plane ride had been silent, with all three of them working away on laptops, trying to find credible threats. When they'd arrived, Connor had tossed gloves at them both. The bacteria survived on surfaces, at least for now, so gloves were needed any time they left a secure facility.

Then the ride in had showed so much devastation already. She swallowed. The streets were empty and several stores already boarded up. The world was hiding from Scorpius.

The guard, an older man with a handlebar mustache, finally allowed them through the door.

Connor lifted his phone to his ear and paused, his face revealing nothing. "Got it. Thanks." He clicked off. "Denver has been quarantined."

"Denver?" Hugh coughed. "The entire city?"

"Yes. Scorpius is taking it out quickly," Connor said, turning away. "All right, experts. Where do we go from here?"

"I'm going to the control room," Ellie said, hefting her laptop over her shoulder.

Hugh nodded. "I want to see the pools, and Connor, how about you check security? Look for problems."

Connor nodded. "Good enough. Remember you're armed for a reason. Scorpius survivors, some of them anyway, go crazy. Really crazy. Something about the bacteria localizing in the brain and stripping empathy. They might try to bite and infect you." He paused, looking them both over. "I didn't even ask. Know how to shoot?"

Hugh rolled his eyes. "I work for Homeland, buddy. And I grew up in the hills of Kentucky, hunting with my brothers. I can shoot." He swallowed and looked at Ellie, his gaze darkening. "But one of us should stay with her."

How sweet. She shook her head. "I've worked for the government for ten years, Hugh. I can outshoot you." Sure, she'd never actually shot a person, but she'd bet her bottom dollar that neither had he. "Let's get to work."

The security guard led her to the main computer room, and she kept an eye out the entire way, kind of wishing Hugh had stayed with her. Her body was warmer in his presence. Always had been. Man, she had to get over this childhood crush she'd had on him. College crush. Whatever. Same thing.

The room held several computer consoles on a metal desk. Beyond the desk was a wide window that looked out on a bunch of equipment. The place smelled of cleanser and metal, and quiet permeated the day.

One lone guy looked up from a computer, his eyes bloodshot, his blond hair slicked back. "Thank God. Reinforcements." His smile lifted pale skin.

"You have a lot of people out sick?" she asked, setting her bag down at a console.

He nodded. "Yeah. About fifty plant-wide. We've disinfected the place like crazy, but you're smart to wear gloves. My name is Lew Jordan."

"Ellie Smithers." She reached for cords to plug in. "I'm a security specialist."

"Sounds good." He turned back to his monitors. "I'm on break in an hour, but if you need anything until then, you just let me know."

"Thanks." Fifty people out were too many. She swallowed. For the first time, she wondered if they'd survive Scorpius. So far, she'd taken a cure for granted. Maybe this really was the big one.

She worked for hours, through Lew's break and after he returned, going through every single system in the facility. Both Hugh and Connor checked in periodically and then went back to their respective jobs. She looked for code, for hacking, for weaknesses. A couple of minor glitches caught her eye, but nothing really concerned her.

Finally, she leaned back and stretched. It had been hours. Lew had brought her lunch, so at least she wasn't starving.

The door opened, and she turned to see a tall man with thick black hair stride gracefully inside.

Lew shoved back from his desk. "Tim. Damn, man, it's good to see you. Where have you been?"

Tim looked around, his gaze clear. "I had to get the family to safer ground but figured I'd better return and help out." He looked down at Ellie from about six feet of height, his face shaven, his jeans and T-shirt clean. "I'm Tim."

"Eleanor." She squinted through her glasses, her eyes gritty. "What time is it, anyway?"

"About ten at night," Tim said, crossing his arms. "I can take over from here, Lew." He didn't take his gaze off Ellie. There was something a little too direct about his stare, and his position blocked any exit.

The hair rose on the back of her neck. "How long have you been gone, Tim?" she asked, trying to sound casual.

"About four days," Lew said, rolling his chair back and standing up. "Too long, but you're here now."

Four days? Long enough to contract and survive the fever. Not everyone who survived went sociopathic, but the odds weren't fantastic. Ellie slowly stretched to her feet, her heart kicking into gear. "I should go find my team."

"I don't think so," Tim said, his teeth flashing in a smile.

Lew paused. "Why? Is something up?" He looked around the room. "We haven't found any threats so far."

"You haven't been looking in the right place," Tim said easily.

"Shit." Lew leaned back. "What are we missing?"

Ellie loosened her arm in case she needed to go for her gun. Truth be told, she was a shitty shot. Maybe she should've practiced more, but she had always had a security detail and computers were more important to her. "I think what your buddy is saying is that he's the threat, Lew." Lew had obviously been existing on way too little sleep.

Lew paused and then snorted. "Seriously. Come on."

Tim nodded. "She's right. Leave, Lew. I want a moment with the smart chick."

Lew straightened, his haggard face sobering. "Wait a minute. Tim? Not you."

"Yeah, me." Tim smiled again. "It was touch and go, but I feel amazing, man. Like nothing can stop me."

Ellie kept her voice low while adrenaline flooded her system. Her legs itched with the need to run, and fast. "This euphoria might be temporary, as are any homicidal thoughts you might be having. It takes a while for Scorpius to finish with the illness." Maybe. Who the heck knew at this point?

"Scorpius?" Lew breathed, wiping off his eyes. "Oh, Tim. I'm so sorry." He brightened. "But you lived. You're okay."

No. Tim wasn't okay. Not at all. Ellie forced a smile. "Yeah. That's great. But you should still be resting."

"I don't need rest." Tim's voice lowered. "Why don't you and I look at the schematics together?"

Yeah. That was going to happen. Wasn't it about time for Hugh or Connor to check in? Ellie really didn't want to shoot this guy. Her hand inched toward her weapon.

"Nope." Tim grabbed a gun from the back of his waist.

A tremor shook her, and the moment narrowed into focus. Her breath sped up.

"Toss your gun over there." He gestured with his.

Ellie didn't move. Losing her gun was a last option.

Tim sighed, turned, and shot Lew in the leg. The sound ripped through the room, amplified by the concrete walls.

Lew screamed and dropped on his ass, both hands instinctively covering the blood bubbling through his jeans above his knee. He gulped out pained sounds.

Ellie jolted and started for the injured man, her mind reeling and her lungs seizing.

Tim turned toward Ellie, keeping the gun pointed at Lew. "Stop. Toss the gun or the next bullet pierces his brain."

Ellie froze.

Lew's agony-filled eyes widened, and he looked at Ellie. His chest heaved and shuddered, but he didn't say a word. Didn't plead for his life. The blood poured between his fingers, coating his hands with red.

Damn it. Ellie drew the weapon out with her thumb and forefinger and set it on the ground, gently kicking it several feet away. She could still dive for it but not before Tim could get off a shot. "You know that Scorpius can make people temporarily crazy, right?" she asked. Or permanently. Who knew at this point?

"I'm not crazy. Just clearheaded for the first time ever," Tim said.

Sweat trickled down Ellie's back. Fear overtook her, and she had to fight to stay in the moment and not mentally retreat. Okay. She'd taken some self-defense classes for work. Eyes and balls. Go for the eyes, the knees, and the balls. But the gun was pointed at her. The fucking gun.

She worked through the angles like the logical scientist she was, forcing reality into her brain. God, she couldn't breathe.

"Tim. What's wrong with you?" Lew gasped, leaning his head back against the wall. His skin had gone eerily pale, making his tortured eyes stand out. "We've been friends for years."

"Friendship and years are overrated." Tim shut the door behind himself.

Ellie sidled a bit to the side, partially blocking Tim's view of the injured man. "Listen. I know you've had a tough time with the bacteria, but you're one of the few to survive. That has to mean something to you." She tried to keep her voice low and calming, but it trembled. A shiver took her and her bones chilled. "Think of the good you can do. To help everyone."

Tim gestured toward her. "I'm thinking of a lot of good I can do. Take off your shirt."

She blinked. What? All right. "No." Then she waited.

His eyebrows lifted. "I have a gun."

Yeah, and if he shot her, he wouldn't get to see her naked. She forced a shrug. "I don't really care." As a bluff, it was the best she could do.

"Ellie? I think we—" The door opened behind Tim, and Hugh started inside, stopping immediately.

Tim rushed forward and grabbed Ellie, yanking her around to face Hugh. She struggled against him, but he shoved the gun against her neck, and her entire body froze. The guy was tall and strong behind her. He held her hip with his left hand and pressed the gun with his right.

Hugh's face lost all expression. He moved closer inside, keeping his gaze on Tim. "I don't think we've met."

"Leave. You need to leave," Tim hissed, his fingers digging into Ellie's hip.

All of a sudden, the good old boy expression was back on Hugh's face. "Well, now. What about the guy bleeding out on the floor? Shouldn't I take him with me?"

"Please, Tim?" Lew moaned. "Don't you remember our friendship a little?"

"I don't care." Tim's voice rose. "Take him. It doesn't matter."

Hugh studied the guy, his blue eyes piercing. "What's your plan, buddy?"

Ellie cleared her throat. "I don't think he has plans with the reactor. Do you, Tim?"

"Maybe. Resources are about to be sparse," Tim said, his voice leveling. "I survived Scorpius. Something tells me I'd survive any amount of radiation that might be spilled."

The guy was nuts. Certifiable. "That's not necessarily true," Ellie whispered. Was there a way to get to him? Her hip was hurting, but the gun against her neck made it hard to breathe. "You mentioned family. Don't you want to get back to them?"

"I lied," Tim said. "My family all died from Scorpius. I'm the only survivor."

"Then be a hero," Hugh said softly. "Let the woman go, and start helping people. Perhaps you were spared for a reason."

Tim chuckled. "I was spared because I'm a god. It's that simple. And now I'm going to take what I want as the world dies."

Hugh's gaze darkened, and he kept it on Tim, above Ellie's head. "A god wouldn't need to hold a gun to a woman's neck. A god wouldn't need to shoot an old friend or scare anybody or even use radiation to harm a community."

"I didn't say I was a good god." Tim snorted at his own joke.

Hugh visibly calculated the situation in a way Ellie remembered well. What was he going to do? She wanted to help, but if she moved an inch, there was a good chance Tim's gun would go off. A tremor shook her and she tried to calm her body.

"Hold still," Tim barked.

"I'm trying," she whispered, her knees shaking.

Hugh took another step toward them. "I think you're a coward, Tim." His tone was low and taunting. "Holding a woman hostage. You're weak. Pathetic." His upper lip curled.

Panic gripped Ellie. What the hell was he doing?

Hugh's snarl grew more pronounced. "I bet you were a wimp before Scorpius."

Tim's body tightened behind Ellie. "You asshole." He turned the gun and pointed it at Hugh, shoving Ellie hard in the side.

Faster than a blink, Hugh whipped his gun out and fired in unison with the maniac.

Ellie screamed and smashed into the wall, her shoulder hitting and then her head. Stars exploded in her vision. The last thing she saw before crashing to the ground was blood bursting from Hugh's shoulder.

Then blackness.

Chapter Five

I might've saved the girl, but I shot a man. Scorpius, whether we've been infected or not…has changed us all.
—Hugh Johnson, Brigade Notes

"Hold on, Ellie." Hugh held her closer to his chest as Connor drove maniacally through the town.

"Want me to hit a hospital?" Connor asked, glancing over at the motionless woman.

Hugh shook his head. "No." Scorpius was rampant in hospitals. "Only as a last resort. She just hit her head."

Connor pressed a button on the dash. "Hey, boss. Hugh got shot."

"You okay?" Deke asked through the speaker.

"Fine. Bullet barely grazed me. I think it has already stopped bleeding," Hugh said.

Connor slowed down and turned. "Was more of a scratch, really."

Felt like a fucking bullet. "Agreed," Hugh said. "Ellie is out." As he spoke, she stirred in his arms, her eyelashes fluttering. Then those stunning blue eyes focused on him. "Hello, beautiful."

Deke cleared his throat. "I'm assuming you're not talking to me."

Ellie blinked. "You shot him," she murmured, seeming to snuggle closer into his chest.

"Shot?" Deke asked.

Connor took another right turn. "We had a problem. Scorpius survivor went nuts and fired at Hugh."

"Is he dead?" Deke asked.

"Yes," Connor said. "Hugh had the better aim."

"The files haven't come in on Gregor or Hugh yet, so I don't know if that's a good thing." Deke sighed. "Status?"

"You're a dick, and I'm perfectly on the right side." Hugh brushed hair away from Ellie's head. "We need to get a better security protocol in place at the power plant. Connor called in reinforcements and they should arrive tomorrow morning."

"Affirmative," Deke said. "As soon as you give them instructions, get on the plane. We need Ellie here at the Pennsylvania power plant."

Ellie sat up in Hugh's lap. "You found something?"

"Maybe." Deke's voice crackled over the speakers. "Somebody has definitely gotten into the computer system, but we need your expertise."

She rubbed her temple. "Email me what you have, and I'll look at it tonight." Then she looked outside at the streetlights flashing by. "I guess I'll look at it as soon as you send it."

"Thanks. Deke out." A click came over the line and then silence.

Connor pulled the SUV into the parking lot of a quaint-looking motel off the main highway. He cut the engine and stepped out, pausing. "Two or three rooms?"

"Two," Hugh answered before Ellie could. She went still in his arms.

Connor eyed her. "Protest now if you don't agree."

She didn't say a word.

Hugh's chest tightened.

"Well, you did save her." Connor nodded and then headed for the office, which had a bright red door compared to the muted blue doors of the rooms.

Ellie turned to meet Hugh's gaze. "What are you doing?"

"You have a concussion probably," Hugh said evenly. "I'm sure there will be two beds, and I won't come near you. But you do need to be observed." Having her soft little body on his lap was pretty much killing him, but he had to watch that concussion.

"Oh." She opened his door and scooted off him, rubbing right across his aching cock.

He bit back a groan.

She stood, waiting a second as her balance took. Then she looked up. "That's too bad. I was kind of hoping we could have sex." Then she turned and strode toward the motel, her sweet ass swaying in her dark jeans.

Sex?

His cock sprang fully awake, and he was out of the car before he could take another breath.

Was she serious?

* * * *

Ellie reached the office just as Connor stepped out and handed her the key to room ten. What the hell had she been thinking? Hugh had promised not to touch her, and she'd just blurted out the first thing she could think of to say. That was so not like her.

Maybe she did have a concussion. In college, he had held all the cards. She had been shy and awkward, and he'd been the freaking star. The guy who hadn't wanted to take advantage of her.

She was a woman now. A successful, strong, adventurous woman.

Holy hell. What had she been thinking to say that to him? Her skin sensitized, and she lowered her chin, moving down the walkway and sliding the key into the slot.

"Wait." Connor ran to the SUV and took two packs out of the back, tossing one at Hugh, who caught it easily. "The hotel manager assured me that they cleanse the rooms every day, but still. We can't be too careful. Wipe down the room before you take off your gloves."

She pushed open the door, more than a little grateful for the leather still protecting her fingers from the damn Scorpius bacteria.

Hugh strode in behind her and unzipped the bag, taking out buckets of antibacterial spray and wipes. It took them almost thirty minutes to completely disinfect the room, and only then did Ellie notice there was only one bed. She stood and stared at it.

"What you said?" Hugh asked when he finished wiping down the small television set. "I know you have a concussion."

She paused. He thought she'd said something outlandish or sexy because she'd had her head bashed into a wall? Humor rippled through her, and she chuckled. So much for being a femme fatale. She turned and looked at him. "You never thought about it? Sex with me?" Curiosity was such a pain in the butt.

His dark eyebrows rose. "Of course I did. All the time."

"Bull," she blurted before she could stop herself.

He straightened to his full height. "I was twenty years old, Ellie. All I thought about was sex. And believe me, you starred in more than one fantasy."

Well. That warmed all her girly parts right up. What was she supposed to do with that information? Then her gaze caught on the belt around his arm. "Holy crap. I forgot all about you getting shot." He'd gotten shot saving her. And he'd killed somebody for her. Although tough, Hugh was a good guy. A nice guy. "I'm sorry you had to kill him."

"Me too," Hugh said, gingerly rubbing his bloody arm.

Just like that, they were back on even footing. They had a job to do, and first was checking out the wound.

A knock sounded on the door and Connor strode inside carrying a first aid kit.

"You're a mind reader," Ellie said, relaxing for the first time in hours, happy she had left the door unlocked for him. Nothing could happen with Connor there, so she could just get over this silly crush and get to work. She dug out her laptop and sat on the bed to open emails from Deke as Connor took care of Hugh's wound.

"It just needs a bandage," Connor said, his voice a low growl. "Or maybe two."

"You're too kind," Hugh said, the tone only slightly sarcastic.

A line of code caught Ellie's eye, and she forgot about the two men. Interesting. Hmmm. She deciphered it, typing quickly, reading each line. "Somebody hacked into the system. Well, probably from the inside. They were looking for employee records and schedules." Squinting, she looked up at the two men. "I need to get to Pennsylvania." She'd be able to do more within the system.

Connor and Hugh worked for a while and then Connor took off for his own room. Sirens filled the night outside—a constant sound since Scorpius had hit.

"I'm taking a quick shower," Hugh said, locking the door and then disappearing into the bathroom.

Ellie found the right code and then paused. She clicked SAVE and sent the information off to Deke. Then she looked at the closed bathroom door.

Hugh had wanted her. Years ago.

She still wanted him.

Life was tenuous at best right now. The pandemic was getting worse, and people were dying daily. Even the ones who lived seemed to be crazy and ending up dead.

She stood.

For years, she'd wondered.

For some reason, she tiptoed toward the bathroom. Was she brave enough to do this? Hell. She might be dead in a week. Or Hugh might. Why play games or be coy or...wait?

Fine. She could do this.

She yanked off her shirt and shoved down her jeans, gingerly sliding into the bathroom buck-ass naked. A semi-clear shower curtain did nothing to conceal the bulk of the man behind it washing his hair. She swallowed.

This was crazy.

But she moved closer to the curtain and whipped it open.

Hugh yelped and tackled her, taking her down to the floor in a move so quick she could only gasp. He flattened her, shoving all the air out of her lungs. His slippery body rubbed against her, and his dick was...right there. Definitely right there.

"Ellie Mae?" He levered up, soap in his hair and dripping down his hard cheekbone.

Oh God. What had she done? His large and soapy body was flush against her nude one. Her nipples hardened instantly. "Surprise?"

He blinked. Once and then twice. He slid a bit to the side, almost off of her, and quickly righted himself with his elbows on the worn bath mat, moving right back into place on top of her.

"You're all soapy," she blurted out. Even his...was soapy.

His brows drew down. "I was in the shower." Instantly, his cock hardened against her. Pulsing. Full. Flattening her clit into explosive sparks.

Oh God. "You're, ah, really hard."

Red tinged his cheekbones. "I wasn't until I landed on top of you." Was he a bit defensive?

A nervous giggle erupted from her chest. "I wasn't accusing you of anything." Then the thought of what she would have been accusing him caught her breath in her chest. "I mean, I could see you behind the curtain. Your hands were up by your head." She had to stop talking. Right now. "Your big head—not the other one. You know. At the top of your shoulders."

She was a moron. A dumbass. Her mouth would never stop.

"Quit talking." He chuckled, amusement lighting his eyes.

"I'm trying," she said.

"Try this." Then his mouth covered hers. Warm and male. She had time for one thought. Oh holy hell, Hugh Johnson was kissing her. Actually *kissing* her.

Then she forgot how to think.

His lips were firm, his movements slow and seeking. Investigating and oh-so-damn tempting. He explored her gently, in control, teasing and stroking. He went deeper, his muscled body pressing her into the floor, his hands at either side of her head and his mouth destroying hers.

Her entire body flashed wild and alive, and an aching need centered in her sex. Finally, he lifted his head, pleasure darkening his spectacular eyes.

The rumors about him in college were true. Beyond true. Hugh could kiss. Really, really kiss. She swallowed, her chest panting against his much harder one. "You can kiss," she murmured.

His lips tipped. "So can you. I always figured we'd be like this."

What was this? Hot and bothered? Needy? She wrapped her hands over his soapy shoulders, letting ripped muscle fill her palms. A soft hum escaped her as she caressed his chest, finally giving in to curiosity and need from so long ago. "I'm on the pill, Hugh."

He hitched against her, and his dick pressed more insistently against her sex. "You blurt out everything in your mind, don't you?"

She nodded. "I'm not much of a game player."

"Ditto." He kissed her again, his chest rubbing against her hardened nipples. "I don't have condoms, but I'm clean. Have to get a physical every year for work."

"Me too." She finally let her hands roam free down his back to slide over his very nice ass.

He grinned and rolled over, bringing her on top of him. "I don't want to crush you."

Unfortunately, he was so soapy she kept right on going and rolled onto the floor, hitting her back against the cold tub.

He winced, reaching for her shoulders. "All right. I'm on top." Then he covered her again.

Warmth surrounded her. Those words. Those silly, simple words.

She wanted them. So she widened her legs, lifting her knees on either side of his. "How about we do this really quickly before one of us breaks something?"

He lifted his head. His blue eyes studied her—full of want and amusement. His hair fell onto his forehead, his still soapy forehead, giving him the look of a rogue. "I can give you fast right now, but then we're taking the night in the bed. The entire fucking night." His dick pressed between her legs as if in perfect agreement.

"Deal," she said, leaning up to kiss him hard on the mouth.

He pushed inside her, going slowly, letting her body accept him.

"Man, you're big," she whispered as her internal walls stretched.

He barked out a pained laugh, setting his forehead against hers. "Don't make me laugh. This might be over too quickly if you do."

She really didn't want that. So she bit her tongue. And then, miracle of all miracles, dream of all dreams…Hugh Johnson was fully inside her.

Finally.

Chapter Six

This is the worst time in the history of the world, or at least in my life, to start something up. But Ellie Mae Smithers is one of a kind. Can we keep it casual? Is that the fates laughing? Damn it.
—Hugh Johnson, Brigade Notes and other shit on my mind

This was beyond insane, and Hugh didn't give a care. He was inside Ellie Mae, and she was every bit as tight, hot, and delicious as he'd known she would be. For the first time in his life, he felt whole.

Now, that was crazy.

Her little body moved beneath his, urging him to get a move on.

Nope. Not this time. Oh, he'd give her faster than usual, but he was still going to destroy her mind. If he was going to lose himself in her, she was going to do the same thing. Plus, she just felt so fucking good.

He lowered his head and kissed her again, a long, deep, rich kiss that took any brain power he had and tossed it out of the steamy bathroom. The shower droned on, and he ignored the sound and the slightly chilling air.

Only her soft breaths and small gasps mattered. They filled him, pouring through his veins.

She tasted sweet and spicy and inherently female. She tasted like hope in a desperate world. More importantly, she tasted like...his. Like he would've known her instantly. "Are you sure, Ellie?" It was a silly question considering he was inside her, but he had to know. Needed to make sure and protect her. He had no choice.

"I'm sure." She lifted her hands and ran her fingers deliciously through his soapy hair. A clump of soap landed on her collarbone, sliding across the small ridge. "Take anything you want, Hugh." Her smile was filled with a siren's edge. "I plan to."

Then she tugged his hair. Erotic tingles lashed down his body to his balls, ramping up his heartbeat and heat.

Had he ever been so aroused? Slowly, he pulled out of her and then pushed back in.

The sound she made stole any control he'd thought he had. Soft little panting with honest need.

She wanted him and had no problem letting him know. He loved that about her. No games, no walls around her heart. She was sweet and smart and honest.

In truth, Ellie was fucking amazing. He had to make this good for her.

Beyond good. "You're beautiful, Ellie Mae," he murmured.

She raked her nails down his sides and grabbed his ass, turning him on enough he started moving faster. Plowing into her. All of a sudden, he went from thought to hunger. There was only Ellie Mae and right here and now. Fire flashed through him. They moved into a wild frenzy, kissing and caressing, their hands all over each other.

He felt eighteen again. Invincible. Desperate.

"Hugh," she moaned. The sounds she made dug into his head, into his heart, planting deep. Her hands were driving him crazy. She clutched at him, rocking to meet his every thrust.

This was Ellie. That one simple thought nearly destroyed him. She was everything.

Tremors started around his cock. Thank God. She arched against him, elongating her neck, crying out his name. The orgasm rocked through her entire body, shaking her breasts against his chest.

Her internal walls gripped him tight.

He exploded, cupping her head and kissing her as deeply as he could, coming with her name on his lips.

Finally, they panted quietly against each other.

He couldn't move. He might not ever move again. The shower continued, the steam abating, the room chilling. Finally, he lifted his head.

Her smile was the sweetest thing he'd ever seen. Her eyes were a satisfied blue, and a lovely pink covered her cheeks. A blob of soap covered her right ear, and soap was spread all over her upper chest. His heart rolled right over.

"So," she whispered, stretching against him. "What now?"

* * * *

Aches and pains—the yummy kind—ran through Ellie's body as she exited the motel bathroom in the morning and stopped short at seeing what was left of the bed. The covers were all on the floor, and even the mattress looked cockeyed.

What a marathon of an evening.

She swallowed. Hugh had gone with Connor to brief the new security team, leaving her lounging in bed after a truly phenomenal night.

The rumors, although awesome, hadn't given Hugh enough credit. He was amazing in bed.

Or maybe her big crush on him helped.

She pushed wet hair off her shoulder and smoothed down her faded jeans. The air had turned cold enough she was comfortable in her light blue sweater. Her phone dinged, and she tore her gaze away from the demolished bed. "Smithers," she answered.

"You alone?" Deke asked without preamble.

"Yes." Striding quickly, she reached her laptop next to the computer and flipped it open, easing back to perch at the end of the bed. "What's up?"

Deke cleared his throat. "The intel came in on Hugh. He's not one of the good guys, Eleanor."

She snorted and inhaled the scent still left in the room from Hugh. Masculine and tough. "He's beyond good." In more ways than one, actually. "You're being silly." Was Deke being overprotective? How loud had they been last night? Had Connor somehow heard something from the next room? She bit her lip. Had she screamed at one point? Geez. "Give me a break, Deke."

"I'm sending you the intel. Call me after you've read it." He clicked off.

Well. She huffed and rolled her eyes, quickly opening an attachment from him. Documents, dossiers, and FBI investigational files quickly filled her screen.

She read them, her stomach beginning to hurt. "This isn't right."

A knock on the door nearly stopped her heart. "Who is it?"

"Connor."

She stood and quickly unlocked the door for him, moving back to her computer instantly.

He slipped inside and leaned back against the door, his dark eyes somber. "I finished at the plant and left Hugh to continue briefing the new security details. Told him I'd be back after grabbing more coffee. Did you read the information from Deke?"

"Not all of it. I'm about halfway through." She didn't believe this. Not at all.

Connor rubbed a hand across his eyes. "Let me fill you in. Hugh's family had financial troubles with what had been very successful tire stores, and Gregor bailed out his brothers. That put Hugh in a world of hurt."

If there was a way to get to Hugh, it'd be through family. She shook her head anyway. "I don't believe this."

"Believe it," Connor said grimly. "Hugh had no choice but to work with Gregor. Fed the guy information on nuclear plants, vulnerabilities, and hot targets. There was a hell of a lot more than just one picture of them together. He really was being investigated by the FBI." His lips pressed into a thin white line as he took in the status of the bed. "Shit, Ellie. You didn't."

She stood, her chest filling. "I did, and he's not a terrorist. Or a co-conspirator with a terrorist organization." The information had to be wrong. It just had to be.

"Read the rest of the files," Connor said softly. "Hugh has been under FBI investigation for the last four months. His vacation? Yeah. That was forced on him, basically so the FBI could go through all of his records at work without his knowledge. He's a bad guy, Eleanor."

No. She'd known Hugh for years. People didn't change that much. They just didn't.

Connor's phone blared out a Florida Georgia Line tune, and he pressed a button, igniting the speaker. "Connor here with Eleanor. What do you want us to do, Deke?"

"Options?" Deke asked, his big voice booming over the speaker.

Connor's rugged face lost all expression. "We can leave him here, bring him with us to answer questions, or put him down and not look back."

Ellie gasped and tossed her laptop on the bed. "We are not putting him down like a dog." There had to be a decent explanation for all of this. "Come on. I know this guy."

"You knew him. Years ago," Connor countered, looking beyond deadly with the gun strapped to his thigh. "It has been about ten years, and a lot can happen in that time. I say we put him down and move on from here. Vet people better in the future."

"No." Ellie moved closer to Connor, almost getting into the big guy's face. "We are going to give him a chance to explain." Her chest hurt. Was she having a heart attack? A panic attack? Yep. One of those was happening right now.

"Deke?" Connor asked quietly.

Silence ticked over the line for a minute. "Fine. Bring him in. But it'll be a lot easier if he's cooperative, so don't let him know we have questions," Deke said.

Connor sighed. "That might be difficult. Apparently, Eleanor and Hugh tore up the sheets last night. Literally."

Embarrassment roared through Ellie and she punched Connor in his rock-hard arm. "Shut up," she hissed. When he glowered, she took a measured step back from the soldier. "I can act normally," she said, her voice only shaking a little bit.

"You slept with him?" Deke barked, his Scottish brogue emerging deep.

"None of your business," Ellie answered, lifting her chin. She wanted to die right then and there. Yep. She sure did.

"It's my business if he's a bloody terrorist," Deke bellowed.

Ellie winced. "He's not." No way in hell. "Now let me get back to the computer so I can figure out what the hell is going on."

Connor glanced down at his phone. "Orders?"

"Bring him in. If he gives you any problems, shoot him," Deke said evenly before clicking off.

Connor shut his phone. "You sure you can do this?"

"Yes." She started typing. There was no way the sweet kid she'd known in college had turned into a terrorist she'd just had the most amazing night of her life with. Hugh had to be innocent.

He just had to be.

Chapter Seven

I'm not sure who's the bigger threat—my friends or my enemies. This world sucks right now.
—Hugh Johnson, Brigade Notes

Hugh settled back in the seat of the private plane, his spidey senses clamoring. Connor had been even quieter than usual as they'd driven to and boarded the plane, which was nearly impossible, and Ellie wouldn't look him in the eye. Was she regretting the previous night?

God, he hoped not. He really wanted to do it again. As soon as possible.

Connor sat behind him, while Ellie sat across the aisle. Within minutes, they were lifting into the sky.

Tension rolled through the interior. He cleared his throat. "How about somebody tell me—" The cool press of metal against his neck stopped his words. What the fuck? "Connor? Any particular reason your gun is against my jugular?" he asked, his own hand inching toward the gun still on his thigh.

"Hand it over, barrel down. Or I shoot you," Connor said, his voice a deep echo behind Hugh.

Hugh eyed Ellie, who was watching with wide eyes. Ah, shit. She looked scared. "No problem." He grasped the gun and held it over his shoulder, where Connor easily took it. "It's okay, Ellie Mae." Why he was reassuring her when she obviously knew what was going on was a mystery he didn't really care to explore.

Something cold and silver encircled his wrist, and within a second, he was cuffed to the chair. "Seriously?" he asked, partially turning to face her after Connor had secured him. "What's going on?"

"We found your file." Connor slapped him almost congenially on the arm and crossed around to face him in the seat in front of him. He smiled, his teeth a white flash against his dark skin. "It looks like I get to use you for target practice."

Hugh sighed, his chest filling. Figured. It just fucking figured. What the hell should he do now? "I'm not dead, so I'm thinking there's a question or two out there." Hopefully.

"No." Connor kicked back, no expression in those hard eyes. "Eleanor argued effectively to keep me from leaving you behind the hotel in a heap of death, so we're bringing you along. It makes no difference whether you push up flowers in Arizona or Missouri. Different flowers, I guess," he mused.

This guy was a bucket of fun, wasn't he? Was he slightly insane? Hugh leaned forward. "Have you survived Scorpius?"

"Nope. I just do what needs to be done," Connor said, his voice a deep baritone. "You might need to be done."

Jesus. "Here I thought we were forming a brotherhood," Hugh murmured, wanting to kick Connor in the head but not wanting to upset Ellie. He cut her a look. "Thanks for keeping him from shooting me in the back."

She gulped and nodded, her eyes huge. "You have some explaining to do."

Connor coughed. "That wouldn't have happened, by the way. When I shoot you, you'll see it coming. I give you my word."

Hugh slowly turned his head to view the soldier. "You're all heart." This guy was colder than cold. Or maybe just messing with him to get information. Either way, Hugh could see how it'd be damn effective.

"So?" Ellie asked. "Explain."

"Explain what?" Hugh asked, his mind spinning. What could he say? Things were too up in the air right now.

"About Gregor. There wasn't just one picture with you and him. And all of those couldn't have been doctored. Tell us about an FBI file that shows you working with him. With helping a terrorist organization," Ellie said, her voice soft. "You have to explain."

He lifted an eyebrow. "You think I'm innocent."

She slowly nodded. "I do."

Ah, the sweetheart. Man, how was he lucky enough to have found her again when he was such a dumbass for letting her go in the first place? "You're a doll, Ellie Mae."

The doll's eyes flared, hot and bright with temper. "Then explain, dickhead. Come on. You're two seconds away from being shot in the head. Work with me here."

He tried really hard not to smile. She was right in that he was probably in deep shit. But she was so damn cute when riled. But he'd taken an oath, and he wasn't going to break it at twenty-thousand feet. Not even for her. "You say we all have top clearance, but I haven't seen it. Prove that you all have the clearance you've claimed, and I'll answer any question you have."

"Did the tire stores have financial troubles?" Ellie asked.

Hugh paused. "Well, yeah. But the economy declined for everyone."

Her brow wrinkled again. Hell, he was worrying her. Would they be able to access his real files? Maybe not. Too many people were out or dead at all the federal agencies. He could tell the truth. But that might not be enough. He sobered. If Deke McDougall decided to shoot him in the head, there really wasn't anybody who could stop him.

Well, shit.

* * * *

Ellie barely kept from smacking Hugh in the nose as he sat at the conference table, looking all calm and reasonable. If the guy had half a brain, he'd be scrambling to make an explanation. Connor and Ivan flanked him while they waited for Deke to arrive.

"It's okay, Ellie Mae," Hugh said, kicking back in the chair.

She sat at the head of the table and gave him a look. "I've been reading the files on you for the entire ride here, and I can't find a loophole. Any sign that you're anything but a crook." It couldn't be true. It just couldn't.

Deke strode into the room. "Well? Are we shooting the bastard?" He yanked out a chair next to Ellie and faced Hugh.

Ellie glanced toward the door. "Where's Nora?"

"On the phone with Lynne Harmony at the CDC. Or rather, at the hospital where Lynne is being treated." Deke didn't look away from

Hugh. "Has he explained?"

"Nope," Connor said, almost cheerfully. "After I shoot him, where are we gonna leave the body?"

Hugh sighed and crossed his arms.

Deke cocked his head to the side. "You're a cool one, aren't you?"

"I'm not." Ellie slapped her hand on the conference table. "Give him your clearance so we can figure this out." She was so finished with the tough guy acts from all the morons at the table and couldn't care less that they were most possibly the most dangerous men in the country right now. "I can't believe the future might hinge on you dorks."

Connor leaned forward enough to see Ivan on the other side of Hugh. "She called us dorks." He sounded slightly hurt.

Deke merely grasped the remote control and brought up several documents on the screen. "Top clearance—for all of us. Even you, Hugh. Because I asked for it, and Homeland gave it to me without checking out your FBI file. Apparently the government is breaking down faster than any of us had anticipated."

Hugh read the documents on the screen. "They look real."

"And since the government is breaking down, nobody is garna come looking for you if you disappear." Deke clicked a button, and the screen went black. "Now's your chance. Talk or Connor is going to start target practice early this week."

Hugh rolled his neck. "When the tire stores started having financial difficulties, I was approached by Gregor Valentino with an offer of a whole lot of money. All I had to do was give him the schematics and maybe a computer code or two for certain nuclear plants in the country."

Ellie closed her laptop to watch his face. Calm. Honest. True. But what the hell was he saying? "And you said no?" she asked.

"I said yes," he said softly, his tone the one he only seemed to use with her. "Before you ask, the Arizona and Pennsylvania plants were included in his list. They're weak, like I told you."

What was he saying? "Hugh," she said, her mind spinning. "You didn't work with terrorists."

"Of course not." He leaned forward and obviously ignored the tensing of the two men on either side of him. "I reported it to my boss, it went up the chain, and all of a sudden I was a fucking double agent. Or spy. Or whatever the hell they're called these days." He ground his palm into his left eye. "I didn't want it, but there it was, and I thought I could do some good. So we've been playing Gregor for about four months."

"And you didn't let the FBI in on your little plan?" Ivan asked, his tone low.

Hugh shrugged. "Not to my knowledge. It's not like the agencies play all that well together."

That was true. Ellie was well aware of that fact. "Who did you report to at Homeland?" She flipped open her laptop.

"Rick Jorgosen," Hugh said.

Ellie did a quick search, and her stomach dropped. "He died a week ago from Scorpius."

"How convenient," Deke drawled. "Anybody else?"

"Hector Gomez," Hugh said, losing his casual look. "He works with Rick."

Ellie typed more. "In a coma in Bethesda. Scorpius." Apparently the bacteria had made its way through that part of the agency rather quickly. Okay. This wasn't looking good. "I can hack into their secure Homeland records, but even with our security clearance, it'll take a while."

"There isn't anybody to flash our clearances at," Deke said with a low growl. "People are dropping like roadkill in spring." His phone buzzed and he lifted it to his ear. "McDougall."

Ellie swallowed and looked around the room. So far, not one of them had been infected. That would probably change at some point. Would they all survive? "I'll find proof for you, Hugh." She knew he was telling the truth, right? A small niggle of doubt entered her head, and she shoved it away. Now was the time for faith, not suspicion. At some point, Deke would tire of waiting. Then what? Would he believe her or just eliminate the possible threat? Now wasn't a time to take risks.

Deke listened to somebody on the other end of the line and then ended the call. Slowly, deliberately, he slipped his phone back into his pocket. "Well."

Ellie's shoulders stiffened. "Well what?"

Deke looked at Hugh. "That was a contact still working at the FBI. Apparently Gregor's body was found a week ago floating in a river in northern Kentucky. Three days after you went on vacation, Hugh."

Hugh flicked his gaze toward Deke. "That's unfortunate."

"Isn't it, though?" Deke asked thoughtfully.

Whoa. This so wasn't good. Ellie dragged her laptop closer. She had to fix this. Either way, she'd get the truth from those files.

God, she hoped Hugh was telling the truth. She couldn't have just slept with a bad guy.

"It's me, Ellie Mae," Hugh said quietly, as if he could read her thoughts.

She looked up and into the blue eyes that still chased her through dreams. It was him. But it had been ten years. Ten long years.

Was he still the guy she'd fallen for so long ago?

Chapter Eight

Sometimes my brain and my heart are at complete odds. Which is neither here nor there for the purposes of this type of journal. So. To get back to it. We've found a credible threat against the nuclear power plant in Pennsylvania, and it's my job to secure Hugh's cooperation. If I don't shoot him first.
—Dr. Eleanor Mae Smithers, Brigade Notes

Ellie nodded at the two armed guards outside Hugh's quarters and then pushed inside without knocking. Each private quarter had been set up like a studio apartment with living area, bed, kitchenette, and attached bath. "Hi."

Hugh sat on the floral sofa with his feet perched on a metal coffee table that housed one pathetic-looking cactus in a chipped red pot. "You here to spring me?"

"No." She moved toward the one available chair, trying like heck to look casual.

"They let you in here by yourself?" he asked mildly.

She blinked and then sat. "I assured them you'd never hurt me." Plus, she knew a few moves. Yeah, it had taken an hour of arguing with Deke, but Hugh didn't need to know about that. "Right?"

Hugh shrugged. "I don't know, Ellie Mae. I could grab you and force my way out of here." If anything, he sounded bored by the entire idea. "Or just take you hostage." His grin was wolfish.

Her face heated. How he could make her blush so easily she'd figure out later. "We need your help."

His eyebrows lifted. "Is that a fact? Your gang thinks I'm a terrorist."

"Nobody really thinks you're a terrorist," she countered, trying hard to sound reasonable and not irritated as hell. "We just need to clear up that undercover op you were on and you'll be fine. But as my code is worming its way into your section of Homeland's computers, before they go down, we need your help."

His bare feet dropped to the floor, and he leaned toward her. "If Gregor is dead, I have no clue who he was working with." Hugh scratched his elbow, somehow looking tough even against the flowered material. "All I got from him those two months was the name of a group called the Haven, or something like that. That's it."

"That's something," Ellie murmured. "I can start there—after I return from Pennsylvania."

He tilted his head to the side. "You're not going to that power plant without me." His tone lost all semblance of lazy playfulness.

Her breath quickened for some inexplicable reason. "I'm afraid you'll have to stay here."

"No." Without seeming to move, he somehow broadened. "That plant is in jeopardy, and I identify threats better than anybody else out there. Even you."

She nodded, wanting to soothe the beast a little. It sucked to be locked up. "I understand, but I'm the computer expert. I can get into their internal servers and maybe find what's going on. At least I need to review the security feeds." She moved to stand.

Quicker than she could blink, she found herself on his lap. He extended his legs again, easily adjusting her into place, his grip firm. "Well, now, here it is," he said, his Southern drawl deepening.

She pushed against his chest, her mind spinning even as desire wound through her. Hard and smooth.

He just tightened his hold, waiting patiently until she stopped wiggling. "Something happened between us last night, Ellie Mae. More than I planned or possibly even wanted. But it's here, and it's fact."

She gaped at him. For years, she'd watched him date girl after girl, woman after woman, and then cheerfully let them go on their way without a problem. Not once, *not once*, had he exhibited one titch of possessiveness. Protectiveness, sure. Kindness and humor, definitely. But not this iron-hard jaw of determination he was facing her with right now. "Have you lost your mind?" she squeaked.

"Quite possibly," he murmured.

What in the world was she supposed to do? This was Hugh, for goodness' sakes. Where was the mellow Southern boy she'd fallen for? "You're freaking me out."

His eyebrows rose. "That's the last thing I want to do." But he didn't release her. "Here's the deal. We went to Arizona—just looking for a threat we actually did not find—and got attacked by a nut job. Your folks, these Brigade experts, say there's a credible threat in Pennsylvania. So you're not going there without me."

Her mouth gaped open.

He gently used two knuckles to tip her chin up.

Her lips met together, and temper stirred at the base of her neck. "Hugh."

"Ellie Mae." He leaned in, his blue eyes suddenly not so mellow. "Scorpius is bad and it's only gonna get worse. I'm not losing you to it. Period."

Well, if that wasn't so sweet, she'd punch him in the nose for being a jackass. But it was a little sweet. Her heart warmed to mingle with her temper.

"Ellie?" Deke's booming voice filled the hallway outside.

She sighed. "Now everyone is calling me 'Ellie.' If one person calls me 'Ellie Mae,' I'm going to kick you." Eleanor was a much more sophisticated and grown-up name, damn it.

He grinned. "Nobody calls you that but me."

The door opened, and Deacan McDougall strode inside. He frowned. "Get off his lap. We need to fly to Pennsylvania. Now."

Ellie unobtrusively pushed against Hugh's thigh…and didn't move. She cut Deke a look.

The massive Scotsman put his hands to his trim hips. "Hugh? Let her the fuck go."

Hugh stood in one smooth motion and turned to face Deke, keeping Ellie tight against his chest. Her hair swung against his face. "I'm the foremost expert in nuclear plant threats right now, and if she's going into danger, I'm going with her," he said.

Deke looked from Hugh to Ellie and back. "Jesus." He shook his head. "What the fuck is this all about? Is this because you knocked boots?"

Knocked boots? Seriously? "That is none of your damn business," Ellie snapped, trying to sound somewhat in control of the situation, which was incredibly difficult considering she was three feet off the ground and cradled against a hard-bodied idiot. "Hugh. Put me down. Now."

With a long, laborious sigh, Hugh set her on her feet. But one broad hand remained on her hip. Solid and secure.

She drew air into her chest and then released it, trying to keep from completely losing her temper. "Hugh comes with us. Period."

Deke's eyes widened slightly. "What did you say?"

"There you go," Hugh said, his voice warm.

She rolled her eyes. "Deke, I understand you don't know or trust Hugh, and that's fine. I'll find those records that clear him. But I do trust him, and we need him on this op. There's a threat against the nuclear power plant, and we don't have time for you guys to dick around. This is serious."

Deke crossed his muscled arms. "I'm in charge."

"Then make the right damn decision," Ellie snapped. "We sought him out for a reason, and that hasn't changed."

Deke smiled then. Slow and threatening. "I guess it'll be just as easy to shoot him in Pennsylvania as here." With that, the Brigade leader turned on his heel and prowled out of the room.

"I think he's really starting to like me," Hugh said, releasing her hip.

She turned and poked him in the chest. Hard. "That was your one chance to act like a bozo. No more, or I'll shoot you myself." Yeah, she might've liked him getting a little possessive over her—nerdy Ellie Mae—but she couldn't let him get away with it long term. "Got it?"

He stepped into her then, his entire long and lean body warm against hers. He gripped her chin, tilting her head back so he could meet her gaze. "I don't remember you being so bossy."

She swallowed, finding breathing a mite difficult. Her body flared wide awake. She tried to speak, and only a croak came out, so she cleared her throat. "Just behave."

His smile was a little lopsided and a lot charming. "Not a chance." Then he kissed her.

Chapter Nine

Why does the world have to start ending when I finally found something worth fighting for? It's enough to drive a man nuts.
—Hugh Johnson, Brigade Notes

Hugh's body finally began to relax as Deke drove the car through town and toward the Pennsylvania nuclear power plant.

The plane ride from Missouri had been stifling, with Connor and Deke arguing about who got to shoot him as soon as Ellie proved he was a terrorist. Finally, Connor had challenged Deke to a rousing game of rock-paper-scissors.

As of nine out of ten, Connor got to shoot Hugh.

It put the soldier in a good enough mood that he hummed all the way from the airport to the plant in the dark SUV. It was nice to make a soldier happy.

Ellie had ignored them all on the plane and had buried herself in some book about masters and mercenaries. Hugh had skimmed the back cover, and whoever author Lexi Blake was, she'd probably spent some real-life time as a soldier. Perhaps she was undercover with Homeland Security as well.

Ivan and Nora had stayed behind in Missouri to work on compiling other crucial threats.

Now, looking around the parking area, Hugh sat in the middle seat with Ellie at one side and Connor at the other. He reached for her hand and took it, surprised again at how small she was. She kept sending him worried glances, so he winked at her.

She blinked twice and then fidgeted in her seat.

"They actually like me a lot," Hugh stage-whispered to her. "All of this posturing is just to stay loose for the op to come."

"Nope," Deke said cheerfully, meeting his gaze in the rearview mirror. "I really want to shoot you. If Connor misses, I get the second chance."

"I never miss," Connor said absently, keeping point out the window.

Hugh grinned. He was actually starting to like these guys. They reminded him of his brothers. He leaned forward to see around Connor. People were bustling on the sidewalks, boarding up businesses and shops. "Looks like everyone is heading to ground for a while."

"Smart," Connor said, his gun resting lightly on his thigh. "Scorpius ain't going anywhere. Getting away from people is a good idea right now."

"You don't think they'll find a cure?" Ellie asked quietly.

Nobody answered. It was unthinkable humans couldn't find a cure to fight a small bacterium, but so far, they'd been losing the war. Hugh tightened his hold on her hand. "They'll find a cure. I'm sure of it." For now, he had a job to do. "After we take care of immediate threats, if the population decreases dramatically, we might need to talk about shutting down these power plants for a while."

It wasn't that easy. But it might be necessary. Was it possible Scorpius would kill that many people?

"One thing at a time," Deke said. "For now, run me through exactly how a nuclear reactor works."

"Sure." Hugh sat back and described the conversion to electrical energy, steam turbines, water reactions, primary coolant systems, and possible targets. He warmed to his subject, impressed by the questions asked by Ellie once in a while.

He always did like smart girls.

Finally, they passed meager security to park in the employee parking lot, which wasn't even half full. More and more people were dropping to Scorpius or just heading out of town. The parking lot led up to an edge with a wide river winding below.

The plant had several buildings and two very large stacks that rose high into the sky. Clouds were slowly forming, but the day was warm enough they didn't need coats.

He followed Ellie out of the vehicle. "Why don't I give you a tour, so you can see what I've been taking about?"

Deke nodded and started for the entrance. "Let's get Ellie to the control room. Ell? I want you to go through the computers and see if anybody has hacked the system. Then please review all security video for the last, what? Say two months. Look for anybody suspicious or who doesn't belong."

Hugh wanted to take her bag off her slender shoulder but instinctively knew her laptop was like another woman's diamonds. She'd want to keep it herself. "Also go through my files, the ones you took, for a list of terrorists or potential threats that I've been watching. Most have Homeland Security photos, so you can compare the two."

"You got it," she said, opening the door and nodding at an elderly guard standing at post.

Well. That was a good sign, at least.

"Let's do this," Deke said grimly.

Hugh paused. "We're not leaving Ellie in the control room alone. She needs cover at all times."

Ellie snorted. "Don't be an ass. I can handle a control room."

His ears heated. There was a fairly decent chance an asshole would try to explode shit at a nuclear power plant in the very near future, and somebody like that would have no problem shooting a lone woman in the head. "She gets a guard, either you or Connor until I'm free, or I sit in there with her the entire time." He glared at Deke. "Your call."

Ellie cut him a look that could slice through concrete.

He glared right back.

Deke rolled his eyes and continued down the hallway. "I told you that you shouldn't have slept with him, Ell."

She made a sound that was kind of like a growl one of his mama's cats had made way back when.

Hugh met her gaze evenly. On this, he wasn't budging.

Connor snorted. "This is going to be interesting."

Hugh's temper heated. Did they really not understand the threat? Fine. "This is now my op."

Deke paused and turned around to face him. He more than filled the hallway with not only size but presence. The Scottish guy was definitely a force all by himself. "Excuse me?"

Hugh set his stance. "Unless any of you truly understand how this place works, and unless you've been tracking nuclear threats for the last five years, you need me. And I just took over the op." Fuck, he hated being in charge. It was too much damn responsibility. But since thousands upon thousands of lives were now in danger, he didn't have a choice.

Especially since Ellie was now in danger, and he could do something about it.

Deke looked toward Ellie, and she shrugged.

Good. There wasn't much any of them could do.

"We are so going to discuss this later," Ellie snapped, her blue eyes burning bright.

Hugh barely kept from wincing. He almost wished they'd find a threat to deal with.

Almost.

* * * *

After a day spent not finding what she was looking for in the computers, Ellie slid her laptop bag across the small table in her motel room, her very late dinner of chicken nuggets settling in her stomach like lumps. Her head hurt, her eyes ached, and her shoulders felt like somebody had shot cement into them with a much too large syringe. She kicked off her shoes, not caring that the carpet had seen better days.

Hugh shut the door behind her. "We need to sterilize the place. Don't touch anything yet."

That was it. That was seriously fucking it.

She whirled around, her hair flying in every direction. "This was a mistake. You and me. Definite mistake." She barely had enough energy to use complete sentences, and she sure as hell didn't have the fortitude to let her temper free. The adrenaline rush might kill her, she was so damn on edge.

He took out a wipe and went to work on the table. "Now, Ellie Mae. You don't mean that."

Why was it the more emotional she became, the more even-keeled and calm he acted? Now that was just a pisser. Her hands clenched. Nothing. She had not one dang thing to throw at his head. Only her phone and a gun at her thigh. She couldn't throw those. Both were needed. "I told Connor to just shoot you," she muttered.

Hugh moved on to the television and furniture holding it. "Yeah. I heard you. At least three times."

"Because you wouldn't leave me alone," she snapped. Why her skin felt too tight and this was bugging her so much, she wasn't sure. But it was. "You don't get to go from casual Hugh in the sack to this overbearing protective looking-to-the-future guy." Oh. That was it. He was throwing her off balance and making her want things that weren't possible. Good. She'd figured it out.

He casually took a spray out of his backpack and took care of the bed, carpets, and even the walls. "I'm not sure what we're going to do when we run out of this stuff."

"The bacteria should be dead by then," she countered, watching him closely. Was he ignoring her words on purpose? "It'll still be in people, but surely we'll have a cure. What the hell is going on in your head?"

He finished the room, returned the spray to his backpack, and concentrated fully on her. "Things have changed."

Warning ticked down her spine. "Not really." No. He couldn't pull this on her. Hugh was a love 'em and leave 'em type of guy. Men like him didn't really change. Especially when a potential apocalypse came calling. "I'm fine with the casual thing you've always had."

"I'm not." He crossed his arms. "I told you that. With you, it isn't casual."

Her heart started to beat faster. This was the worst time in the entire timeline of humanity to start a real romance. Well, except during the plague. No. Scratch that. This was worse. Especially since she now had a beyond dangerous job, and he seemed hell-bent on protecting her. There was no protection these days.

There was a whole lot of planning and even more luck. That was it. "You need to take a breath."

His grin was oddly determined. A little intimidating. How strange. Especially since the look he gave her sent little tingles through her entire lower body.

"I'm breathing just fine, baby. I understand you're scared," he said.

"I'm not scared," she retorted like any eight-year-old challenged on the playground. She cleared her throat, trying to look like an adult, damn it. "I'm just being realistic."

"I'm not gonna hurt you, Ellie Mae," he said, his voice gentle. "Not you. Feel free to fall hard."

She blinked. Once and then twice. Was that arrogant? She mulled it over, watching his implacable face. Wait a minute. Hell yes, that was arrogance. "While I like confidence as much as the next girl, give me a break. You're not that irresistible." Yeah, right. She was getting better at this whole lying thing, though.

He pressed his lips together, and it took her a second to realize he was trying not to chuckle.

What an ass. Her phone was in her pocket. She could throw it. He'd probably catch it. But then that wasn't worth the risk of breaking the device. Her chest tightened. "I am not falling at all." Man, that was a lame response.

He gave up the pretense and just smiled.

Somebody knocked, and he opened the door so Conner could poke his head in. "We're getting some shut-eye before returning to the plant early to secure the remaining areas. Deke said to tell you if you leave, he'll hunt you down and slice the skin from your body, Hugh."

Irritation itched through Ellie. "Go away, Connor. I am still working on those files to clear Hugh's name." Though if Deke didn't believe in Hugh's innocence, Hugh would probably already be dead. "Go to bed."

Connor winked and then shut the door.

Quiet descended. Ellie cleared her throat. "So. My rules. Either we keep this casual, or you need to find another room."

He moved toward her then. One long and smooth roll of pure maleness with a side of grace and intent.

She took a step back. What the heck? If he could play her way, they could really take the edge off. Just being in the same room with Hugh sent her nerves all a-fluttery, and that just had to stop. Her nipples hardened.

He reached her, sliding both palms down her arms. "Your rules, huh?"

"Yes." She lifted her face toward his.

His blue gaze darkened. "No."

Then he kissed her.

Chapter Ten

I guess maybe starting a romance during a pandemic—possibly the *pandemic—isn't that crazy. What am I saying? That's insane! But it's Hugh. I'm thinking he's worth the risk. Oh, on a business level. We're closing in on whomever hacked into the Pennsylvania system to learn the systems. I hope.*
— Dr. Eleanor Smithers, Brigade Notes

Ellie barely got out a gasp before Hugh deepened the kiss. His force pushed her head back, which conveniently fit right into his big palm. He held her in place, his mouth beyond devastating.

There was an edge to him, to his touch, that hadn't been there before.

The clock was counting down on all of them, maybe on all of the world. But here, in this moment, there was only the two of them.

Finally.

His lips pressed down on hers, and it was like she'd never stopped wanting him—even after college. She kissed him back, her tongue meeting his. While she'd imagined this, with him, the reality was so much bigger than her fantasies.

Her heart raced. Desire rippled through her, and her nipples tightened even harder against his chest.

Never in her life had she wanted anybody or anything more. Hugh Johnson. He released her enough to let her breathe and slid his tongue over her lower lip. Her knees trembled, and need exploded inside her abdomen.

He leaned back, looking down at her. His strong and chiseled face was set in harsh lines. Desire, a dark hunger, glimmered in his eyes.

Without warning, he lifted her up and pushed her against the wall. The breath whooshed out of her lungs, and she grabbed his chest to keep balance. God, she loved his easy strength. She should be getting his agreement about keeping this casual, even if that's not what she wanted.

No sane woman would want merely casual with this guy. But it was all he'd offered anybody in the past. And the future looked dismal for pretty much the entire world.

She blinked and tried to think of words. Her body was splintering apart. "Hugh."

"Forget the world. Forget fears and threats," he rasped, the tone of his voice licking right along her skin. "Stay with me. Right now."

God, she wanted him. Wanted to forget the threats around them and just fall into this heat. Passion and need consumed her.

"I want you. So bad it's nearly impossible," he murmured, one broad hand brushing her hair away from her face, even as he kept her pinned against the wall.

Had anybody ever wanted her this badly? If so, she couldn't remember.

And she was on fire. The fierce lust in his eyes was burning her alive, and she had never needed like this. Could this be healthy? "Hugh. Now." They had way too many clothes on.

He easily ripped her shirt over her head, and she lifted her arms, letting him take her bra with it. No way would he let her fall. Her shirt flew over his shoulder, and she grabbed his, yanking up. He ducked his head to help.

Then all of that smooth skin over hard muscle was in her hands. She moaned, running her palms across his strong chest.

He set her down and released her jeans, taking them to the ground in one smooth motion. With indulgent gentleness, he lifted her again, setting her bare ass on the clean table. The fake wood was cold against her skin, which had heated beyond reason. She grasped his bunched biceps to keep from falling back. "Hugh?"

He leaned in, and she felt the rough touch of his fingers on her inner thigh. Electricity zapped through her. She arched toward him, needing more. So much more. Getting lost in him, forgetting the horrible reality they all lived in, felt almost as good as his touch.

She craved him. Right here and right now. To wipe fear away and just live.

His fingers moved beneath the edge of her panties. She shut her eyes, and small sparks lit behind her eyelids. Material ripped, and then two of his fingers pushed into her sex.

She arched, biting her lip. It felt too damn good. But she needed more. "Hugh. Now."

"You're just getting ready." Amusement and need darkened his tone as he stroked her. "And I've been dreaming of this for a decade." Dropping to his knees, he manacled her thighs and drew her toward his mouth.

She fell back onto her elbows, her hair brushing the table.

This was decadent. Was the door even locked? The walls were thin, too.

Her thighs trembled. "I think that maybe we should go to the bed?"

"No. I deserve a treat, and you need to be ready for the night I have planned." Then he licked her, his tongue swirling around her clit.

God. The rumors about him in college had been true. He was a master at this.

She let her head fall farther back.

His shoulders kept her open and exposed for him. He hummed softly against her clit, fucking her with two fingers. "Ah, baby. So sweet. And you are getting ready. All swollen and wet just for me."

Her thighs quivered more.

An orgasm built inside her, roaring close.

"Try not to yell too loud," he said, his heated breath torturing her clit. "They'll come running in to see what the problem is."

She groaned and bit her lip but couldn't move. She was so damn close.

His big, callused fingers were killing her. She tried to dig her nails into the worn table and tightened her body. He worked her faster, his tongue magical, his fingers knowing just where to stroke.

Tension coiled inside her, driving up her need. He nipped her clit and she detonated, arching completely and moaning his name. He licked her, his fingers trapped inside as her sex clamped around them.

Her inner muscles trembled forever. Then she slowly came down.

God. "That was incredible." She lowered her chin just as he lifted up, his gaze meeting hers between her thighs. It was the most intimate position she could even imagine, and yet, Hugh looked right. She smiled. "Your turn."

He didn't return the smile.

She sat up, and he helped her. Her hair tumbled over her shoulders, and heat filled her face. His erection was definitely straining against his worn jeans. She reached out and ran a finger down his hard length.

He sucked in air, his ripped abdomen muscles clenching.

She reached for his zipper.

"Wait." He grabbed her hands, trapping them. "I can't go on just pretending this is what it is. I don't want to leave things like this, believe me, but I need more, Ellie Mae."

She blinked and looked up at him. "What?"

He ran a finger down her cheek. "I've reached a point where I'm all or nothing. With you. Only you."

What was he saying? "Hugh? The world is exploding." Emptiness gnawed at her. She wanted him inside her. Now.

He nodded. "I know. But I'm a selfish bastard when there's something I want, and I want you. For as long as I can have you. If you say yes tonight, yes to more, then we're giving this thing a real chance. Hearts and flowers and all that shit."

Her heart raced into motion. It was more than she'd even let herself dream about. Tension arced between them. "Okay." There were probably better words. More emotional ones.

But that one seemed to do it for Hugh.

He lifted her by the waist and walked to the bed, ripping back the covers and setting her on the sheets. Red stained his high cheekbones, his chiseled features showing hunger. For her.

No matter how long she lived, she'd never forget that look in his eyes. That look just for her.

"I'm keeping you, Ellie Mae." He pushed her back and flattened his big body over her, covering her with heat and muscle.

She widened her thighs, wanting more of him. "I'm keeping you," she whispered.

He pushed inside her. "There's no going back."

Who the hell would want to? She scored her nails down his back, digging them into his hard ass. He pulled out and pushed back in, the muscles in his arms bunching near her head.

Sparks and fire and undefinable need filled her, taking over every nerve. She grabbed his arms for balance and tried to meet his thrusts.

He powered harder into her, going deeper than she would've thought possible.

A quaking started deep inside her, sweeping out and stealing her breath. She arched and exploded, waves rippling through her with a primal orgasm.

He dropped his head to the crook of her neck and came, his entire body shuddering.

She swallowed. Whoa. Okay. Wow.

Slowly, he levered up and smiled, satisfaction glimmering in his eyes. "Now that was a good start, Ellie Mae."

Chapter Eleven

It's too late to just grab Ellie and head for the hills. Now we have to save the world, one threat at a time. Damn. It just figures the apocalypse would mess with my plans.
—Hugh Johnson, Brigade Notes

Hugh strode back into the motel room and tossed a bag of breakfast burritos toward Ellie, who sat on the bed, mumbling to herself as she typed away on the laptop. "Deke and I found an open fast-food joint." There weren't many left at the moment, unfortunately.

She nodded and set the laptop to the side. "My program finally found the time the computers were searched. While you were gone, I compared the time with the security feed, and found the guy who'd messed with the computer. I'm pretty sure." She reached for the bag of food. "He isn't one of the employees of the plant. I've been through all of their pictures and employee files."

Man, she was smart. And nicely glowing after their marathon the previous night. He leaned over and kissed her, taking his time. She tasted like sweetness and hope.

A pretty blush covered her face.

"I meant every word last night." It was only fair to make sure she fully understood that.

She lifted an eyebrow. "I'm well aware."

That was true. They did know each other. He grinned and took the laptop, flipping it around to see the screen. A bomb dropped into his gut. "This is the guy?"

She paused in unwrapping a burrito, her eyebrows raising. "Yeah. Why? Recognize him?"

"Yeah." Hugh wiped a hand across his eyes. Yusef had grown a longer beard, but his angled features were familiar, as were his dark eyes. He looked shorter with the thick boots and dark pants than Hugh remembered. "I've been watching him for a while." Hugh grimaced. "Call Deke and Connor. If this guy somehow got inside, we have a bigger problem than we thought."

Ellie grabbed her phone and quickly texted. Within seconds, Deke and Connor walked inside, both still munching on burritos. "Hugh knows the name of the guy I have on video working on the computer," she said.

Connor dropped into a chair at the table, and Deke leaned back against the door.

"Where is he now?" Deke asked grimly.

Ellie shook her head. "No clue, but I emailed his picture to Nora and Ivan. Ivan is going through all the traffic cams and security cameras in the area around the power plant. He'll report in if he sees this guy at any point."

Hugh blew out air. "The guy's name is Yusef Masih. He's around twenty-five and was here on a student visa a year ago to study computer science in graduate school." Hugh tried to remember the details. "But he went back to Saudi Arabia and was taken off my radar."

"Why was he on your radar initially?" Deke asked.

"Alleged association—based on a street informant and not any emails, texts, or personal contact—with one of the suicide bombers at the Bellevue marathon two years ago," Hugh said. Three people had died in that attack. "But neither Homeland nor the FBI could tie him close enough to the perpetrator, who was a Seattle born man named Franklin Belamy."

Deke nodded. "I know the case. But somehow this guy is back in the states and has now basically walked into a nuclear power plant and used the computer."

Ellie winced. "Too many people died or are dying so quickly. We haven't had proper security measures in place to deal with a pandemic like Scorpius."

Hugh eyed the picture. "To the best of my recollection, Yusef has no training with explosives or nuclear energy." He looked at the young man's photograph. "We did hack into his computer, and he had done some research on explosives. But it looked like he was studying both computers and mechanical engineering. When his visa expired, he left the country."

"Yet he's back," Ellie muttered.

"Yes." Without raising any flags for Hugh, which was a red flag. "If he's planning an attack on a nuclear plant, he has help. His background doesn't lend itself to this."

"Except for the computer part," Ellie murmured.

"What did he get?" Deke asked.

She shook her head. "Not much. Just the employee records, schedules, and schematics of the plant. The schedules aren't even in place now."

"Can he cause problems from the computer standpoint?" Deke asked.

Ellie twisted her lip. "No. Even without people, there are computer safeguards in place that should last for a couple of years, at least. Even if he hacked the entire system, which is incredibly difficult if not impossible, there are safeguards upon safeguards."

Hugh nodded. "It'd be much easier to just get inside and plant bombs. Especially around the spent fuel." It had always been his biggest nightmare.

Deke's phone buzzed, and he lifted it to his ear. "McDougall." His straightened to his full height, his face going hard. "When? You sure? Thanks." He clicked off. "That was Ivan. He caught Yusef Masih on camera several hours ago near the plant."

Hugh stiffened. "We have to get there. Now."

Ellie jumped up and reclaimed her laptop. "I need my gun."

Hugh paused. "You're not going. Not in a million years."

* * * *

Ellie paused, taking a second to let Hugh's words sink in. "That's sweet and all, but if they have messed with the computers, I'm needed." She liked having him worried about her, but this was life or death. She ran a hand down his arm. "Hugh. Think about it. If they succeed and blow up that waste, we're all dead anyway."

He blanched. "Geez."

Yeah.

"Suit up," Deke ordered. "We leave in one minute." He paused. "I've read your file, Johnson. You're trained with explosives as well."

"Of course," Hugh responded. "This has always been the threat, Deke."

Ellie studied him. She hadn't known that. Hugh always had been much more complex than most people saw. She grabbed her gun to strap to her thigh.

Connor and Deke ran out of the room.

Hugh finished securing his weapon and then drew her close, holding her tight. She slid against him like she'd always been there. His masculine scent and warmth surrounded her. "Be safe," she whispered, her voice muffled against his chest.

His heart was thundering against her cheek. "You be safe. I ain't losing you now."

She blinked back tears. While she was trying to be brave, her bones felt frozen. Her chest hurt. They might not survive the day. She leaned back her head. "We'll be okay."

He gently kissed her. "I know." Then he took her hand and led her out of the room. They jumped into the back of the SUV, where Connor and Deke already awaited. Deke roared away from the hotel. "So. I guess you guys don't want to shoot me yet," Hugh said.

Deke shrugged. "Might not be an issue."

Oh yeah. Ellie coughed. She opened her laptop and brought up her second search. Files flittered across the screen. The program had taken longer than she'd thought. She sighed, finally finding the info she'd needed. File after file of Hugh's undercover op from the top brass at Homeland. "Here's the proof that Hugh was always working with Homeland." Well. Considering they were all probably about to die, that was a bit anticlimactic. Then she snuggled closer to him.

Connor took the laptop and read. "Could be faked."

Hugh chuckled, the sound strained. Even he wasn't immune to the nuclear threat they were about to face.

Ellie reached out and punched Connor in the arm. "Knock it off."

Deke sighed. "Is it clear and concise?"

"Yep," Connor said, handing the laptop back. "We'll have to find another reason to shoot him."

The casual banter was going to kill her. This was beyond insane.

They were headed toward a nuclear power plant that was probably about to be bombed. She shivered, and Hugh drew her closer. There were so many words she'd never gotten to say to him. She lifted her head, and he quickly kissed her.

"It's going to be okay. I promise," he whispered.

She nodded, even though he couldn't make that promise. Nobody could anymore.

They reached the security gate and passed through. Nobody was there.

"This isn't good," Connor muttered. He glanced over his shoulder. "We're gonna need those plans to shut down these types of places for a while. Well, after we deal with today's threat."

Hugh stiffened against Ellie. "It's not that easy."

Of course it wasn't.

Deke pulled into a parking spot. "Guns off safety." He jumped out of the SUV and strode for the door.

Ellie's shoulders relaxed a tiny bit upon seeing a guard at the front door. A young, sweating guard.

Deke eyed the kid and handed over his credentials. "This your post?"

The kid looked at the badge and shook his head, handing it over. His brown security uniform was stained, and his brown eyes earnest. "No, sir. I usually patrol the back fence. But I called in about an hour ago, and nobody was here, so I figured I'd better watch the door."

Deke clapped him on the back. "Smart man. Just do your job." He motioned for the rest of the group to follow. "Anybody could've gotten in during the last hour. Hugh? What's the plan?" He kept moving at a quick clip.

Hugh kept Ellie to his left. "I'll take Ellie to the computer room and do a quick scan of the security recordings. See if anybody looks suspicious. Deke, you go check out the waste pools."

"Copy that," Deke said, veering left. "What am I looking for?"

"A bomb," Hugh said tersely. "Anything that shouldn't be there."

Deke started jogging and yelled back. "Everyone keep your phones close."

Hugh nodded, hustling Ellie toward the control room. "Connor? Remember where the cooling system is?" he asked.

"Affirmative," Connor said.

"Go look for explosives there," Hugh said. "I'll be along after I check out the security."

Connor took a sharp right turn down a cement hallway.

Sweat trickled down Ellie's back, even though it wasn't hot. "I can't believe this," she muttered.

"Ditto." Hugh yanked open the heavy door to the computer room.

Ellie's heart hitched. The room was completely empty. "We're losing to Scorpius," she whispered.

"Right. That's okay. We'll deal with that later." He motioned her toward the main area. "We have to bring up the security feed. Right now, let's deal with this threat."

"Good plan," said a voice across the room. Yusef Masih rose from behind a cabinet, gun out and pointed at them. "It will be a pleasure to kill you today."

Ellie dropped her laptop.

Hugh froze and then crossed in front of her. "Run, Ellie. Get help."

"No." She reached for her gun.

"Drop it or I'll shoot him," Yusef yelled.

She bit her lip. "Why are you doing this?" Who would do such a thing?

"Gun," Yusef said, spittle spraying from his mouth. His eyes were a wild hue. "Now."

Hugh gingerly reached for his gun and set it on the floor. "Ellie. It's okay."

Her hand shook, but she did the same, stepping away from the gun with her hands up.

Yusef glared. "I guess I do not truly need to wipe the security feed. Soon there will be nothing left here but rubble."

The muscles in Hugh's shoulders and back bunched. "Remember what I told you."

What?

He backed into her, turned, and all but shoved her toward the door with his hips.

"Stop it," Yusef ordered.

"No," Hugh said softly. "I'm one of those lucky guys who sees things clearly." Reaching behind his back, he yanked open the door. A quick twist of his hips, and he put Ellie outside. "Run, Ellie!" he yelled, leaping across the room toward Yusef.

A gun went off. The door slammed shut.

Bullets impacted the door. She ducked and ran down the corridor, yanking her phone out of her pocket and dialing Deke. "Deke! Get back, quick." Then she turned and kept low, heading back to the computer room.

There had to be a way to save Hugh.

How badly had he been shot?

Keeping her head down, she all but crawled back to the door and tried to open it. Nothing. She partially stood and used all her strength.

Damn it. They'd locked it?

She tried to remember the schematics of the place just as Deke came running up.

He tried to open the door with no luck. "What the hell?"

"There's another entry," Ellie said, looking frantically around. "We have to get in there. Now."

Chapter Twelve

Why are some people so fucking crazy?
—Hugh Johnson, Brigade Notes

A hard slap to the face brought Hugh into consciousness. Pain exploded in his right shoulder. He opened his eyes and tried to focus.

Huh? What the hell?

He shook his head and then winced as invisible needles poked his eyes from inside his head.

"There you are. Wake up, dickhead," said a rough voice.

Focus, damn it. Hugh zeroed in on the voice and then the face surrounding it. Deep blue eyes, brown hair liberally streaked with gray, trimmed beard. Dark eyebrows. Gray sweater. Northern USA type of accent. "Who the fuck are you?"

The guy smiled. "You aren't dead."

Hugh tried to move and then realized he was tied to a chair—nowhere near the control room of the nuclear power plant. How had they moved him? He looked around. He sat in a chair in what looked like a metal storage facility. Yusef sat in another chair over in the corner, typing into a tablet. Against the opposite wall, a stunning redhead with green eyes watched Hugh impassively, her perfectly manicured hands at her hips.

"Where am I?" Hugh asked. His head pounded with strong hammer strokes.

"To answer your questions, I'm Orion, and this is a temporary stop," the guy said, pulling up another metal chair so they were almost knee to knee. "Or your grave, I guess."

Well, fuck. Hugh looked at his right shoulder, not surprised to see blood all over his shirt. He'd gotten hit again? "You shot me, asshole," he said mildly to Yusef.

The guy didn't even look up from his tablet.

"He doesn't talk much," Orion said.

Hugh squinted a little, feeling lightheaded. "But you do. What the hell was your name?" His brain was fuzzy.

"Orion," the guy said.

Hugh snorted. "That's freakin odd. Very."

"I earned it the hard way," Orion said, his voice a low rumble. The more he talked, the more he sounded like a native Kentuckian.

Huh. This guy was nowhere near Hugh's radar and had never been. "You attacked the plant?"

"Yep." Orion smiled, flashing perfectly tended white teeth.

"I've never heard of you."

Orion nodded. "I've stayed away from notoriety. Just prepping for the opportunity."

Prepping? Had he just said "prepping?" Hugh frowned. "Like those guys who store food and ammunition in the woods, pretending to be soldiers?"

"We're not pretending. Just waiting for an opportunity created by God," Orion said.

Wait a minute. Hugh slowly shook his pounding head. "You're an apocalyptic prepper. Seriously? One just waiting for a chance to harm people."

Orion leaned back. "No. Of course not."

What the hell was happening? "Did I hit my head?"

"Yes. After you got shot. It was hell getting you out of the plant before your friends caught up with us," Orion said. "They really should vacate the premises now."

Shit. Ellie. Hugh struggled against the restraints, biting back pain as his shoulder protested. Vehemently. "Okay. Let me get this straight. You're a terrorist because you've been given the opportunity?" Why was the world so cloudy? How hard had he hit his head, anyway?

Orion rubbed broad hands down his dark jeans. "No. I've been prepping and getting ready for the apocalypse for some time. After studying the issue, I've determined that the only way my people will survive is if we cut down on competition for meager resources."

Nausea rolled in Hugh's gut. "So you're killing a hundred thousand people and making this area unlivable? That makes sense to you?" He glanced at the woman.

She looked to Orion. "He knows what he's doing. Orion will save us all."

Jesus. "You're stuck in a cult, sweetheart," Hugh muttered, shaking his head. "This is ridiculous." He leaned to the side to see Yusef, the guy who had once really been on Hugh's radar. "How'd you get back into the country, anyway?"

"He had help," Orion said. "The man knows his way around computers, so I recruited him. But he doesn't really believe in our calling. Our paths just converged." Casually, almost slowly, Orion pulled a gun from his boot and pressed it to his knee. "I told him he could kill you when we were done chatting."

"I do love a good chat," Hugh said calmly, trying not to puke. This man was freaky nuts. "Had some training, have you?"

"Most of us at the Haven have."

Hugh blinked. "The Haven. I've heard of you." When he'd been undercover. Gregor had mentioned the group. So they really did exist. As a prepping cult preparing for the apocalypse. Life just kept getting weirder.

Orion's eyebrow rose. "That's interesting. I thought we'd been silent."

Hugh swallowed, his throat feeling parched. "Nobody is that silent." Yet he'd never heard of this guy.

"I brought you here for some answers. So you've heard of the Haven but not of me." Orion frowned and leaned forward, pressing a thumb into Hugh's wound. "What have you learned?"

Hugh groaned as pain flew down his arm. His heart stuttered. "You're from Kentucky, aren't you?"

The man's eyes hardened. "No. Boston."

Lie. That was definitely a lie.

Hugh shook his head, trying not to pass out. Blackness crawled in from the distance, and his vision wavered. "Get your fucking thumb out of my flesh."

Orion sat back and wiped his thumb off on Hugh's jeans. "That was kind of grotesque. Just answer my questions so I don't have to do it again."

"Fuck you."

The woman giggled. Not laughed. Not chuckled. Giggled. "He's tough."

Orion cut her a smile. "He's about to lose consciousness again. Not so tough." He leaned in. "How did you know about this particular threat? What clue did we leave?"

Admitting it was just statistics, and luck wasn't going to get Hugh anywhere. He glanced at Yusef and then back. "Maybe your allies don't really believe in your cause. You know?"

Orion stiffened. "What are you saying?"

"You tell him, Yusef," Hugh called out. "Let's just say that you're not his only ally. In fact, you're not even in his top ten." Shit. This was a total bluff. What the hell did Hugh know?

Orion looked over his shoulder as Yusef glanced up from his tablet. "Yusef?"

The younger man met Orion's gaze evenly. "He is manipulating you. I have not told anybody about you or the Haven."

Orion looked back at Hugh.

Hugh shrugged. "I heard about the Haven from a gun runner who's good buddies with Yusef. When there's information that needs to be traded, this guy doesn't have your back, Orion." He could sense distrust. What he hoped was distrust. It might just be his desperation to live that was messing with him. "Why don't you just shoot him?"

Orion studied Hugh, not looking too bothered by the idea. "How did you know about the plant here being a target? I didn't tell anybody until we arrived."

So much for sowing the seeds of distrust. Hugh rolled his eyes. "Where else would you hit?"

"Arizona," Orion said instantly.

Hugh coughed. Was that blood in his mouth? Was he bleeding internally? No. A shoulder wound wouldn't do that. "Yeah, I thought about Arizona, too. Better casualty rate in Pennsylvania. Easier to get to from the east coast, too."

Orion nodded. "That's what I thought."

So the bastard's headquarters was on the east coast somewhere. Or could it be back in Kentucky? There was game to eat and water to drink. Hills to hide in. Orion wouldn't be near a major city. Not as a prepper.

"You know, I've studied threats for years. Real ones," Hugh murmured, his head almost lolling on his shoulders.

"Yeah?" Orion asked.

"Yeah. And not once did I think I'd have problems with homegrown prepper terrorists." Weren't most preppers off living in mountains and squirreling away food and medical supplies, just wanting to be left alone? "Not once."

The woman against the wall looked at her watch. "Orion? We should probably get going. The HMX is supposed to detonate soon."

HMX? "Where the hell did you get that shit?" Hugh tried to narrow his focus. Man, his head fucking hurt. Worse than his shoulder, actually. HMX was a plastic explosive more powerful than C-4. Damn it. He blinked and tried to send the pain somewhere else. He had to figure out how much time Ellie had. "How much HMX?"

"Enough to spread radiation far and wide," Yusef said, still typing. He chuckled quietly.

Hugh kept his focus on Orion. One lunatic at a time. "How many explosives were set? Or do you even know?"

"He's trying to manipulate you," the woman said, looking kind of like a sleek cat.

"I know, Wanda," Orion said. "It's okay. Hugh Johnson of the DNDO probably has some training in interrogation. Not what you have, of course."

Ah shit. They'd taken his wallet. "What do you have, Wanda?" Hugh asked. The more he found out about this nutty trio, the better. Assuming he survived this.

"Plenty," she murmured, her voice educated and cultured. While she wore a dark sweater and jeans, her boots looked shiny and expensive. What Hugh knew about fashion could fit in an egg cup, but the woman looked like money. Odd for a prepper. "I also know that we really must get going. My understanding of the radiation radius is that we're running out of time." She moved to the closed roll-down door and waited.

Orion patted Hugh on the leg. "I'm sorry we can't talk longer. I have many questions for you."

"We can bring him with us," Wanda said.

"No," Yusef said, finally setting down his tablet. "I get a personal kill today. You gave me your word."

Orion stood. "That I did. We'll meet you at the border." He chucked Hugh almost good-naturedly on the chin and kept on walking, easily lifting the door. Only another closed door across the hallway was visible. "Good-bye, Hugh." He took Wanda's arm and escorted her out of sight.

Hugh set his feet inside the legs of the chair. They'd tied his wrists to the metal but not his ankles. "Why you want me dead, Yusef?" Hugh asked, gingerly trying to see if his injured shoulder still worked at all.

Yusef stood and took off his glasses, placing them on his chair along with his tablet. "Your military causes more deaths abroad than you can know. We're tired of it."

"How about you and I start a dialogue right now about that?" Hugh asked, wincing as his shoulder pulled. He needed to focus through the pain and forget fear. There was only now.

"There's not time. Your people are blowing up a nuclear power plant." Yusef drew a knife from his back pocket. Double edged and military issued, the blade gleamed in the dim light. "Just think of the damage."

"I am," Hugh said softly. "You can't really align with that moron Orion."

"No. He's just a means to an end. And he's not that stupid." Yusef took another step closer. "You should see the way his people follow him. Blindly and with total conviction."

Hugh braced his knees. "How about you and I get out of here and go stop the bomb? Save a hundred thousand people?" And Ellie. God, he had to save Ellie. His gut churned and sweat burned into his eyes.

"No." Yusef drew ever nearer. "Have you ever sliced another man's jugular?"

"No," Hugh said, tilting his head to the side. "Have you?"

Yusef just shrugged. Then he struck.

Hugh waited one second and then leaped up, turning and smashing the chair into the oncoming man. Yusef went down. Hugh leaped around and dropped, his knees slamming on either side of Yusef's neck.

A fast twist and a balance on the chair, and Yusef's neck snapped.

Hugh panted and staggered to his feet, letting the body drop. For years, he'd trained in hand-to-hand, just in case. "I didn't want to kill you." He spoke the absolute truth.

Quiet came from outside.

He looked around for anything to get the damn chair off his back. Time was running short.

He had to get to Ellie.

Chapter Thirteen

I've never been so scared in my entire life as when I got into that computer room and Hugh was gone. Life has changed so much, and I fear it's just getting started.
—Dr. Eleanor Smithers, Brigade Notes

Ellie ran through the hallway and followed the blood just in time to see two men load an unconscious Hugh into a van. She tried to run after them, and Deke stopped her with an arm around her waist. "Let me go," she yelled, her body shaking.

"Later." The soldier forced her back inside and put her to the wall. "Eleanor. Listen to me."

Panic heated down her body, seizing her lungs. She couldn't breathe. "Deke. We have to get him."

Deke's eyes softened even as his jaw hardened. "We will. But first things first. Those guys did something, and we have to figure out what it was and then fix it. If this place goes, we're all dead. Along with thousands upon thousands of other people."

She gulped in air and tried to stop crying. Okay. Her hand shook. She wiped her face. Deke was right. "I need the security feeds."

Deke took her arm while bringing the phone to his ear. "Ivan? Hugh just got taken from the power plant. Hack into any and all cameras and track him. If you need satellites, contact General Boseman. Nora has the number." He clicked off. "We'll get Hugh back. I promise."

She wiped more tears away and ran back to the computer room. "I can go in reverse with the security feed from right now and track that guy. The one who shot Hugh." She sat and started typing, bringing up video. How badly had Hugh been shot? It seemed like there had been a lot of blood. God. Was he okay? Why had they taken him? It had to be for information about this mess or even other nuclear power plants.

Deke leaned over to see over her shoulder. "Keep going."

They watched the video in reverse, switching camera angles every few minutes.

"Wait. There." Deke pointed to the screen. "Slow down."

Ellie slowed the video and then stopped breathing. Yusef had entered one of the other buildings, climbed stairs, and stood over huge pools of nearly luminous blue waste. It was oddly compelling. "Hugh was right. Isn't that the spent fuel?"

Deke straightened. "Yeah, and that's a bomb." He breathed out and moved for the door. "Keep watching and make sure they didn't plant any other explosives. Let me know as soon as you do."

Ellie glanced up, her body chilled beyond cold. "What are you going to do?"

Deke shoved open the door. "Find Connor and figure out how to defuse this bomb." He grimaced. "I don't know shit about explosives." Then he disappeared down the corridors.

Ellie turned back to the video. There couldn't be any more explosives. Right?

She traced Yusef's movements from the time he'd arrived at the facility until he'd taken Hugh. Her heart sped up as she watched the feed of Yusef meticulously planting two big bundles of explosives around the nearly luminous blue waste pools, just like Hugh had predicted. The bomber had worked alone.

Then her breathing just up and stopped when he planted a third bomb behind what looked like a bunch of equipment above the pool.

Then he exited and made his way to the computer room, where he'd run into Hugh.

God. She had to tell Deke about the third explosive. She launched herself at the door, ripped it open, and barreled right into Hugh.

She bounced back, and he grabbed her arms to keep her from falling. "Hugh." She jumped right back into his warmth, her chest bursting. "God. You're okay." Tears pricked her eyes. Wait a minute. She leaned back and grabbed his right arm. He'd tied what looked like a bunch of rope around the wound, and it was already turning red.

His eyes were clear, though. "I'm okay. You?" He almost frantically ran his good hand down her arm.

"Yes." She gulped, finally getting centered at seeing him standing in one piece. "You're okay. I wanted to come get you—"

"There's at least one bomb." He kissed her quickly on the forehead and tried to push her toward the exit. "I'll go find it. Get to the car."

Not a chance. She grabbed his hand and started running down the hallway toward the facility containing the waste storage. "He planted three explosives in boxes with locks, and one is hidden. We have to get to Deke."

"Shit." Hugh took the lead, running through hallways and down corridors, outside, and to the storage facility. He led her inside and up two flights of steel stairs.

He paused at seeing Deke and Connor hunched over a box next to another box with the pools below them, bright and blue. "How bad is it?"

Deke glanced up. "Shit if I know. It has a combination lock. We could break it open, but I don't know how volatile this thing is. You?"

Hugh edged forward and crouched to check out the bomb. He gingerly grasped it.

"Whoa," Connor said, standing to his full height. "What if you joggle it or something?"

Hugh lifted the box and looked under it. "We're good. There has to be a timer or a detonator that they'll hit as soon as they're out of range, and I can't see how much time we have. But they should be to safety already, so any second this could go off. Grab the other one."

Deke shrugged and gingerly grasped the box, holding his breath.

"There's a third box." Ellie ran around the equipment and grasped the final box. Her hands were shaking. "What now?" She backed away from the giant blue pool of death.

"This way." Hugh turned and jogged around the railing back the way they'd come. "It's plastic explosives. Won't go off if you run. So fucking run." He launched into a faster movement.

Ellie held her breath and ran after Deke, her heart thundering. She had a damn bomb in her hands. This was insane. The air whooshed out of her and she sucked more in, conscious of Connor on her right.

"Do you want me to take it?" he asked.

"No." She shook her head, afraid to move it more than she already was. Her footsteps pounded down the corridors after Hugh until they burst into the parking lot. Shocking rain splashed into her. When had it started raining?

Thunder rolled high and loud above them.

"This way," Hugh bellowed, running for their SUV. He gently placed his box on the floor in the back. "Keys." As Deke winced and put his box next to Hugh's, Hugh grabbed the car keys out of his jeans' pocket. Then he turned and took Ellie's box to slide on the seat. He slammed the door shut.

Ellie grabbed his arm. If they were going to blow up the SUV, they should really run.

He kissed her hard and then jumped into the driver's seat. "Love you, Ellie Mae."

"Wait—" Deke grabbed the door handle, but Hugh hit a button and locked it. The engine ignited. Hugh punched the gas pedal, and the SUV swerved and then gained speed, heading for the river.

Ellie yelled for him, her body going numb. Shock? Stress? A way to avoid pain?

The SUV sped up and then arced, sailing right over the embankment toward the rushing water. "Hugh!" she screamed, bursting into motion and running across the asphalt. "Did he jump?"

"Don't know," Deke said, running right alongside her.

They reached the edge.

The SUV hit the water with all four windows down and slowly sank.

Ellie tried to scramble down the bank but Deke held her back. "Wait a minute."

The earth seemed to still. Then the SUV, only partially under water, exploded.

* * * *

Hugh rolled over on the grassy bank, smashing into a tree. He covered his head as the explosion threw water, car parts, and a couple of fish high into the air. Smoke and debris plumed up. The water burst in every direction, rolling all the way up to his boots.

Then silence.

He gasped in air, his heart thundering. The rain pelted down and he rolled over, letting it wash over his face. God. This was nuts.

Slowly, he shoved to his feet and looked up. Just trees.

His entire body hurt. Head to fucking toes.

He limped between trees, following a barely-there path and finally emerging at a small stone path with stairs. Ellie was already running down them with Deke ineffectually trying to grab her arm.

Upon seeing him, Deke halted.

Within seconds, Ellie Mae was against him. The pain was worth it. Hugh put his good arm around her and kissed her wet hair. "It's okay, Ell."

She shoved him. Hard. "What the holy fuck were you doing?" She backed up, her face wet, fury in her eyes. God, she was beautiful. Those blue eyes were deep enough to get lost in forever. "You don't tell somebody you love them and then go crash an SUV full of bombs into a fucking river." She was yelling now. Had a good set of lungs on her.

"Underwater explosions don't propel objects through the water as far as surface explosions," he gently explained. "It's the drag water exerts on objects."

She hit him in his good arm. Hard. "I know that. I got an A in chemistry, remember?" Tears were sliding down her face.

"Ah, baby? I think you're in shock." Hell. He might be, too. An interesting ringing had set up between his ears. He moved for her and then ducked back when she tried to hit him again. If he remembered right, she wasn't that great of an aim. If she hit his injured arm, it'd drop him.

Connor jumped down the stairs. "Hugh, man." He reached him, gingerly plucking a stick out of Hugh's waist. Blood flowed out of somewhere near his ribcage and trickled down his jeans. "You, um, might need stitches."

Hugh grinned as the world started to tilt in what should be an alarming manner. "Yeah. Hey. We're friends now."

"We surely are." Connor caught him in strong arms right before he hit the ground. Now that was a good friend.

Chapter Fourteen

My first week on the job wasn't so bad. I got shot, had a concussion, ended up needing several stitches, and prevented an explosion from causing spent nuclear fuel to burn and throw radiation across the land. Oh. And I fell in love with my Ellie Mae.
—Hugh Johnson, Brigade Notes

Hugh kicked back in his Missouri quarters, contentedly eating some vanilla ice cream that Nora had so kindly brought to him after he'd been all stitched up. He sat on the flowery couch with his feet up on the dented coffee table. The bed was behind him, the kitchenette to his right, and a small television on a table in front of him. How long would they have television?

Most of the plane ride home was a blur, but now he was rather content. Where was Ellie, anyway?

A knock sounded on his door. "Come in." He licked his spoon. There she was.

Nope. Connor strode inside, still wearing a leather duster that made him look like a badass. "Came to check on you." He hovered near the sofa.

Hugh gestured to the seat. "You can stay."

Connor grinned, his teeth a flash of white in his dark face. "No way. Ellie will be finished debriefing Nora soon, and she's pissed, man. I mean, *pissed*."

Hugh paused in his ice-cream eating frenzy. "She's mad? Really?"

Connor's eyebrows rose. "Hell, yeah. I've never seen her like this."

He patted Hugh's healthy shoulder. "But I think you're awesome, brother. Great job today."

Hugh grinned. "You, too. This is going to be quite the ride, isn't it?"

Connor gave him a look. "Yeah. I'm glad you have my back."

"Ditto." Hugh meant it. Connor was a hell of a soldier. It was nice to bond.

"All right. I'm out of here before she arrives," Connor chuckled, turning and all but jogging for the door.

Some brother. Hugh smiled. This was a good place, and these were good people.

Ivan poked his head in the door, his eyes a piercing blue. "Is Ellie here yet?"

"No." Hugh motioned him in. "You're welcome, though."

Ivan glanced behind him. "That's ah, all right. I'll come back later. I'm glad you're okay." He smiled and then disappeared.

Huh. The intelligence specialist was afraid of sweet Ellie? Interesting.

The door shoved open, and Hugh straightened, relaxing upon seeing Deke stride inside. "Hey. You done debriefing?"

"Not yet," Deke whispered, his green eyes sober. "I just wanted to check on you. Great job today, man. I'm glad we brought you on board."

Hugh frowned. "Why are you whispering?"

Deke straightened to his full and rather impressive height. "I'm not," he whispered.

Hugh shoved the spoon into the ice cream carton. "Don't tell me you're scared of Ellie."

Deke's eyes widened. "Nope. Just wanted to make sure you were doing great. I'll see you tomorrow." The dangerous soldier backed to the door, gingerly slid outside, looked both ways, and then made a run for it.

Hugh swallowed. Okay.

The door opened again, and sweet Ellie Mae stood there. Her thick hair bounced around her shoulders, and her stunning eyes shot sparks.

He tried not to wince.

"I cannot believe you drove toward a river with bombs in the car." She moved toward him, her hips swaying in a very nice way. "That was insane. Dumber than dumb. Did you have a lobotomy in the ten years we were apart?"

Man, she was lovely. "No." He set the ice cream on the table by the sofa. "I'm, um, sorry I scared you."

"Scared me?" Her voice rose about fifteen octaves. "Scared me. You're sorry you scared me."

He nodded.

"Not good enough." For once, her cheeks weren't pink. They had bloomed a very angry red. "Not even close."

"You're right."

"I am. I love you, Hugh Johnson. I mean it. Forever. No more bombs."

Her words were a hit to the chest. She loved him. He tried not to smile, because even though she'd said what he wanted to hear, she was still obviously furious with him. Fuck, this was confusing. He tried to move and then winced.

Her face softened just a little. Was that concern? Hell yes. He'd totally run with it. He gingerly patted his newly stitched abdomen and then leaned forward. "I'm so sorry, Ellie Mae," he groaned, pouring it on thick. "Let me come talk to you." He let his breathing hitch.

"No." She rushed for him, settling him down and sitting next to him. "Don't move."

"Well, okay." He wrapped his good arm around her and drew her close. Yeah. She'd ended up right where he wanted her.

She caught his satisfied gaze. "Oh. You did not."

He tried to look injured. Truth be told, Nora had given him a very nice pain killer. "I love you, Ellie Mae."

* * * *

Those three words just melted right through Ellie, as he no doubt planned. She pressed her palm against his very sure and strong heart. "You said there was no going back," she said softly.

He covered her hand with his. "I did say that. Meant it, too."

She snuggled into him, her body still rioting. "Then no more messing with bombs. Next time, we figure out a safer way to be…safe." They were silly words, especially considering the world was dying from a pandemic, but she needed them. Needed to somehow hold on to the thought that they'd survive. Together. "I need you, Hugh."

He ran his palm down her arm, giving comfort and reassurance. Yeah. He knew how hard those words were for her to say. When she'd lost her mom, she'd lost all family.

Now she had him and the rest of the Brigade gang. They were family. All she had. "I've already started searches for Orion and that Wanda woman you talked about. More danger is coming. You can't take chances like that," she said.

He gently eased her onto his lap, straddling him. His blue eyes, so dark and fathomless, caught her gaze. "I promise to be more careful because nothing is going to take me away from you, sweetheart." He stroked down her face. "I waited a long time for you. I'm not going to let you get away now."

Her heart turned right over. He was solid and sure beneath her. All of him. The crush she'd had in college had grown into something strong. Real and everlasting. "I waited longer for you."

His grin was a little lopsided. "I never was as smart as you. So that makes sense."

She chuckled.

He leaned up, capturing her mouth. His kiss was sweet and sexy, slow and sure. Definitely all Hugh. "I love you, Ellie Mae. For as long as we have."

She leaned into him, caressing his jawline. "We'd better have forever, Hugh."

He kissed her again. "I promise."

* * * *

Also from 1001 Dark Nights and Rebecca Zanetti, discover Tangled, Teased and Tricked.

Sign up for the 1001 Dark Nights Newsletter
and be entered to win a Tiffany Key necklace.

There's a contest every month!

Go to www.1001DarkNights.com to subscribe.

As a bonus, all subscribers will receive a free copy of
Discovery Bundle Three
Featuring stories by
Sidney Bristol, Darcy Burke, T. Gephart
Stacey Kennedy, Adrian Locke
JB Salsbury, and Erika Wilde

Discover 1001 Dark Nights Collection Five

Go to www.1001DarkNights.com for more information

BLAZE ERUPTING by Rebecca Zanetti
Scorpius Syndrome/A Brigade Novella

ROUGH RIDE by Kristen Ashley
A Chaos Novella

HAWKYN by Larissa Ione
A Demonica Underworld Novella

RIDE DIRTY by Laura Kaye
A Raven Riders Novella

ROME'S CHANCE by Joanna Wylde
A Reapers MC Novella

THE MARRIAGE ARRANGEMENT by Jennifer Probst
A Marriage to a Billionaire Novella

SURRENDER by Elisabeth Naughton
A House of Sin Novella

INKED NIGHT by Carrie Ann Ryan
A Montgomery Ink Novella

ENVY by Rachel Van Dyken
An Eagle Elite Novella

PROTECTED by Lexi Blake
A Masters and Mercenaries Novella

THE PRINCE by Jennifer L. Armentrout
A Wicked Novella

PLEASE ME by J. Kenner
A Stark Ever After Novella

WOUND TIGHT by Lorelei James
A Rough Riders/Blacktop Cowboys Novella®

STRONG by Kylie Scott
A Stage Dive Novella

DRAGON NIGHT by Donna Grant
A Dark Kings Novella

TEMPTING BROOKE by Kristen Proby
A Big Sky Novella

HAUNTED BE THE HOLIDAYS by Heather Graham
A Krewe of Hunters Novella

CONTROL by K. Bromberg
An Everyday Heroes Novella

HUNKY HEARTBREAKER by Kendall Ryan
A Whiskey Kisses Novella

THE DARKEST CAPTIVE by Gena Showalter
A Lords of the Underworld Novella

Discover 1001 Dark Nights Collection One

Go to www.1001 DarkNights.com for more information

FOREVER WICKED by Shayla Black
CRIMSON TWILIGHT by Heather Graham
CAPTURED IN SURRENDER by Liliana Hart
SILENT BITE: A SCANGUARDS WEDDING by Tina Folsom
DUNGEON GAMES by Lexi Blake
AZAGOTH by Larissa Ione
NEED YOU NOW by Lisa Renee Jones
SHOW ME, BABY by Cherise Sinclair
ROPED IN by Lorelei James
TEMPTED BY MIDNIGHT by Lara Adrian
THE FLAME by Christopher Rice
CARESS OF DARKNESS by Julie Kenner

Also from 1001 Dark Nights

TAME ME by J. Kenner

Discover 1001 Dark Nights Collection Two

Go to www.1001 DarkNights.com for more information

WICKED WOLF by Carrie Ann Ryan
WHEN IRISH EYES ARE HAUNTING by Heather Graham
EASY WITH YOU by Kristen Proby
MASTER OF FREEDOM by Cherise Sinclair
CARESS OF PLEASURE by Julie Kenner
ADORED by Lexi Blake
HADES by Larissa Ione
RAVAGED by Elisabeth Naughton
DREAM OF YOU by Jennifer L. Armentrout
STRIPPED DOWN by Lorelei James
RAGE/KILLIAN by Alexandra Ivy/Laura Wright
DRAGON KING by Donna Grant
PURE WICKED by Shayla Black
HARD AS STEEL by Laura Kaye
STROKE OF MIDNIGHT by Lara Adrian
ALL HALLOWS EVE by Heather Graham
KISS THE FLAME by Christopher Rice
DARING HER LOVE by Melissa Foster
TEASED by Rebecca Zanetti
THE PROMISE OF SURRENDER by Liliana Hart

Also from 1001 Dark Nights

THE SURRENDER GATE By Christopher Rice
SERVICING THE TARGET By Cherise Sinclair

Discover 1001 Dark Nights Collection Three

Go to www.1001DarkNights.com for more information

HIDDEN INK by Carrie Ann Ryan
BLOOD ON THE BAYOU by Heather Graham
SEARCHING FOR MINE by Jennifer Probst
DANCE OF DESIRE by Christopher Rice
ROUGH RHYTHM by Tessa Bailey
DEVOTED by Lexi Blake
Z by Larissa Ione
FALLING UNDER YOU by Laurelin Paige
EASY FOR KEEPS by Kristen Proby
UNCHAINED by Elisabeth Naughton
HARD TO SERVE by Laura Kaye
DRAGON FEVER by Donna Grant
KAYDEN/SIMON by Alexandra Ivy/Laura Wright
STRUNG UP by Lorelei James
MIDNIGHT UNTAMED by Lara Adrian
TRICKED by Rebecca Zanetti
DIRTY WICKED by Shayla Black
THE ONLY ONE by Lauren Blakely
SWEET SURRENDER by Liliana Hart

Discover 1001 Dark Nights Collection Four

Go to www.1001DarkNights.com for more information

ROCK CHICK REAWAKENING by Kristen Ashley
ADORING INK by Carrie Ann Ryan
SWEET RIVALRY by K. Bromberg
SHADE'S LADY by Joanna Wylde
RAZR by Larissa Ione
ARRANGED by Lexi Blake
TANGLED by Rebecca Zanetti
HOLD ME by J. Kenner
SOMEHOW, SOME WAY by Jennifer Probst
TOO CLOSE TO CALL by Tessa Bailey
HUNTED by Elisabeth Naughton
EYES ON YOU by Laura Kaye
BLADE by Alexandra Ivy/Laura Wright
DRAGON BURN by Donna Grant
TRIPPED OUT by Lorelei James
STUD FINDER by Lauren Blakely
MIDNIGHT UNLEASHED by Lara Adrian
HALLOW BE THE HAUNT by Heather Graham
DIRTY FILTHY FIX by Laurelin Paige
THE BED MATE by Kendall Ryan
PRINCE ROMAN by CD Reiss
NO RESERVATIONS by Kristen Proby
DAWN OF SURRENDER by Liliana Hart

Also from 1001 Dark Nights

TEMPT ME by J. Kenner

About Rebecca Zanetti

Rebecca Zanetti is the author of over forty romantic suspense and dark paranormal novels, and her books have appeared multiple times on the New York Times, USA Today, BnN, iTunes, and Amazon bestseller lists. She has received a Publisher's Weekly Starred Review for *Wicked Edge*, Romantic Times Reviewer Choice Award for *Deadly Silence* and Nominations for *Forgotten Sins* and *Sweet Revenge*, and RT Top Picks for several of her novels. Amazon labeled Mercury Striking as one of the best romances of 2016 and Deadly Silence as one of the best romances in October. The Washington Post called Deadly Silence, "sexy and emotional." She believes strongly in luck, karma, and working her butt off...and she thinks one of the best things about being an author, unlike the lawyer she used to be, is that she can let the crazy out. Find Rebecca at: www.rebeccazanetti.com

Discover More Rebecca Zanetti

TEASED
A Dark Protectors—Reece Family Novella
By Rebecca Zanetti

The Hunter
For almost a century, the Realm's most deadly assassin, Chalton Reese, has left war and death in the past, turning instead to strategy, reason, and technology. His fingers, still stained with blood, now protect with a keyboard instead of a weapon. Until the vampire king sends him on one more mission; to hunt down a human female with the knowledge to destroy the Realm. A woman with eyes like emeralds, a brain to match his own, and a passion that might destroy them both—if the enemy on their heels doesn't do so first.

The Hunted
Olivia Roberts has foregone relationships with wimpy metro-sexuals in favor of pursuing a good story, bound and determined to uncover the truth, any truth. When her instincts start humming about missing proprietary information, she has no idea her search for a story will lead her to a ripped, sexy, and dangerous male beyond any human man. Setting aside the unbelievable fact that he's a vampire and she's his prey, she discovers that trusting him is the only chance they have to survive the danger stalking them both.

* * * *

TRICKED
A Dark Protectors—Reese Family Novella
By Rebecca Zanetti

He Might Save Her
Former police psychologist Ronni Alexander had it all before a poison attacked her heart and gave her a death sentence. Now, on her last leg, she has an opportunity to live if she mates a vampire. A real

vampire. One night of sex and a good bite, and she'd live forever with no more weaknesses. Well, except for the vampire whose dominance is over the top, and who has no clue how to deal with a modern woman who can take care of herself.

She Might Kill Him
Jared Reese, who has no intention of ever mating for anything other than convenience, agrees to help out his new sister in law by saving her friend's life with a quick tussle in bed. The plan seems so simple. They'd mate, and he move on with his life and take risks as a modern pirate should. Except after one night with Ronni, one moment of her sighing his name, and he wants more than a mating of convenience. Now all he has to do is convince Ronni she wants the same thing. Good thing he's up for a good battle.

Tangled
A Dark Protectors—Reece Family Novella
By Rebecca Zanetti

Now that her mask has finally slipped…
Ginny O'Toole has spent a lifetime repaying her family's debt, and she's finally at the end of her servitude with one last job. Of course, it couldn't be easy. After stealing the computer files that will free her once and for all, she finds herself on the run from a pissed off vampire who has never fallen for her helpless act. A deadly predator too sexy for his own good. If he doesn't knock it off, he's going to see just how powerful she can really be.

He won't be satisfied until she's completely bare.
Theo Reese had been more than irritated at the beautiful yet helpless witch he'd known a century ago, thinking she was just useless fluff who enjoyed messing with men's heads. The second he discovers she's a ruthless thief determined to bring down his family, his blood burns and his interest peaks, sending his true nature into hunting mode. When he finds her, and he will, she'll understand the real meaning of helpless.

Vampire's Faith
By Rebecca Zanetti

The Dark Protectors are back on June 19, 2018 with Vampire's Faith!

Vampire King Ronan Kayrs wasn't supposed to survive the savage sacrifice he willingly endured to rid the world of the ultimate evil. He wasn't supposed to emerge in this time and place, and he sure as hell wasn't supposed to finally touch the woman who's haunted his dreams for centuries. Yet here he is, in an era where vampires are hidden, the enemy has grown stronger, and his mate has no idea of the power she holds.

Dr. Faith Cooper is flummoxed by irrefutable proof that not only do vampires exist . . . they're hot blooded, able to walk in sunlight, and shockingly sexy. Faith has always depended on science, but the restlessness she feels around this predatory male defies reason. Especially when it grows into a hunger only he can satisfy—that is if they can survive the evil hunting them both.

* * * *

Chapter 1

Dr. Faith Cooper scanned through the medical chart on her tablet while keeping a brisk pace in her dark boots through the hospital hallway, trying to ignore the chill in the air. "The brain scan was normal. What about the respiratory pattern?" she asked, reading the next page.

"Normal. We can't find any neurological damage," Dr. Barclay said, matching his long-legged stride easily to hers. His brown hair was swept back from an angled face with intelligent blue eyes. "The patient is in a coma with no brain activity, but his body is... well…"

"Perfectly healthy," Faith said, scanning the nurse's notes, wondering if Barclay was single. "The lumbar puncture was normal, and there's no evidence of a stroke."

"No. The patient presents as healthy except for the coma. It's an anomaly," Barclay replied, his voice rising.

Interesting. "Any history of drugs?" Sometimes drugs could cause a coma.

"No," Barclay said. "No evidence that we've found."

Lights flickered along the corridor as she passed through the doorway to the intensive- care unit. "What's wrong with the lights?" Faith asked, her attention jerking from the medical notes.

"It's been happening on and off for the last two days. The maintenance department is working on it, as well as on the temperature fluctuations." Barclay swept his hand out. No ring. Might not be married. "This morning we moved all the other patients to the new ICU in the western addition that was completed last week."

That explained the vacant hall and nearly deserted nurses' station. Only one woman monitored the screens spread across the desk. She nodded as Faith and Dr. Barclay passed by, her gaze lingering on the cute man.

The cold was getting worse. It was early April, raining and a little chilly. Not freezing.

Faith shivered. "Why wasn't this patient moved with the others?"

"Your instructions were to leave him exactly in place until you arrived," Barclay said, his face so cleanly shaven he looked like a cologne model. "We'll relocate him after your examination."

Goose bumps rose on her arms. She breathed out, and her breath misted in the air. This was weird. It'd never happen in the hospital across town where she worked. Her hospital was on the other side of Denver, but her expertise with coma patients was often requested across the world. She glanced back down at the tablet. "Where's his Glasgow Coma Scale score?"

"He's at a three," Barclay said grimly.

A three? That was the worst score for a coma patient. Basically, no brain function.

Barclay stopped her. "Dr. Cooper. I just want to say thank you for coming right away." He smiled and twin dimples appeared. The nurses probably loved this guy. "I heard about the little girl in Seattle. You haven't slept in—what? Thirty hours?"

It felt like it. She'd put on a clean shirt, but it was already wrinkled beneath her white lab coat. Faith patted his arm, finding very nice muscle tone. When was the last time she'd been on a date? "I'm fine. The important part is that the girl woke up." It had taken Faith seven hours of doing what she shouldn't be able to do: Communicate somehow with coma patients. This one she'd been able to save, and now a six-year-old girl was eating ice cream with her family in the hospital. Soon she'd go home. "Thank you for calling me."

He nodded, and she noticed his chin had a small divot—Cary Grant style. "Of course. You're legendary. Some say you're magic."

Faith forced a laugh. "Magic. That's funny." Straightening her shoulders, she walked into the ICU and stopped moving, forgetting all about the chart and the doctor's dimples. "What in the world?" she murmured.

Only one standard bed remained in the sprawling room. A massive man overwhelmed it, his shoulders too wide to fit on the mattress. He was at least six-foot-six, his bare feet hanging off the end of the bed. The blankets had been pushed to his waist to make room for the myriad of electrodes set across his broad and muscular chest. Very muscular. "Why is his gown open?"

"It shouldn't be," Barclay said, looking around. "I'll ask the nurse after you do a quick examination. I don't mind admitting that I'm stymied here."

A man who could ask for help. Yep. Barclay was checking all the boxes. "Is this the correct patient?" Faith studied his healthy coloring and phenomenal physique. "There's no way this man has been in a coma for longer than a couple of days."

Barclay came to a halt, his gaze narrowing. He slid a shaking hand through his thick hair. "I understand, but according to the fire marshal, this patient was buried under piles of rocks and cement from the tunnel cave-in below the Third Street bridge that happened nearly seven years ago."

Faith moved closer to the patient, noting the thick dark hair that swept back from a chiseled face. A warrior's face. She blinked. Where the hell had that thought come from? "That's impossible." She straightened. "Anybody caught in that collapse would've died instantly, or shortly thereafter. He's not even bruised."

"What if he was frozen?" Barclay asked, balancing on sneakers.

Faith checked over the still-healthy tone of the patient's skin. "Not a chance." She reached for his wrist to check his pulse.

Electricity zipped up her arm and she coughed. What the heck was *that*? His skin was warm and supple, the strength beneath it obvious.

She turned her wrist so her watch face was visible and then started counting. Curiosity swept her as she counted the beats. "When was he brought in?" She'd been called just three hours ago to consult on the case and hadn't had a chance to review the complete file.

"A week ago," Barclay said, relaxing by the door.

Amusement hit Faith full force. Thank goodness. For a moment, with the flickering lights, freezing air, and static electricity, she'd almost traveled to an imaginary and fanciful place. She smiled and released the man's wrist. "All right. Somebody is messing with me." She'd just been named the head of neurology at Northwest Boulder Hospital. Her colleagues must have gone to a lot of trouble—tons, really—to pull this prank. "Did Simons put you up to this?"

Barclay blinked, truly looking bewildered. He was cute. Very much so. Just the type who'd appeal to Faith's best friend, Louise. And he had an excellent reputation. Was this Louise's new beau? "Honestly, Dr. Cooper. This is no joke." He motioned toward the monitor screen that displayed the patient's heart rate, breathing, blood pressure, and intracranial pressure.

It had to be. Faith looked closer at the bandage covering the guy's head and the ICP monitor that was probably just taped beneath the bandage. "I always pay back jokes, Dr. Barclay." It was fair to give warning.

Barclay shook his head. "No joke. After a week of tests, we should see something here that explains his condition, but we have nothing. If he was injured somehow in the caved-in area, there'd be evidence of such. But... nothing." Barclay sighed. "That's why we requested your help."

None of this made any sense. The only logical conclusion was that this was a joke. She leaned over the patient to check the head bandage and look under it.

The screen blipped.

She paused.

Barclay gasped and moved a little closer to her. "What was that?"

Man, this was quite the ruse. She was so going to repay Simons for this. Dr. Louise Simons was always finding the perfect jokes, and it was time for some payback. Playing along, Faith leaned over the patient again.

BLEEP

This close, her fingers tingled with the need to touch the hard angles of this guy's face. Was he some sort of model? Bodybuilder? His muscles were sleek and smooth—natural like a wild animal's. So probably not a bodybuilder. There was something just so male about him that he made Barclay fade into the *meh* zone. Her friends had chosen well. This guy was sexy on a sexy stick of pure melted sexiness. "I'm going to kill Simons," she murmured, not sure if she meant it. As jokes went, this was impressive. This guy wasn't a patient and he wasn't in a coma. So she indulged herself and smoothed his hair back from his wide forehead.

BLEEP

BLEEP

BLEEP

His skin was warm, although the room was freezing. "This is amazing," she whispered, truly touched. The planning that had to have gone into it. "How long did this take to set up?"

Barclay coughed, no longer appearing quite so perfect or masculine compared to the patient. "Stroke him again."

Well, all righty then. Who wouldn't want to caress a guy like this? Going with the prank, Faith flattened her hand in the middle of the guy's thorax, feeling a very strong heartbeat. "You can stop acting now," she murmured, leaning toward his face. "You've done a terrific job." Would it be totally inappropriate to ask him out for a drink after he stopped pretending to be unconscious? He wasn't really a patient, and man, he was something. Sinewed strength and incredibly long lines. "How about we get you out of here?" Her mouth was just over his.

His eyelids flipped open.

Barclay yelped and windmilled back, hitting an orange guest chair and landing on his butt on the floor.

The patient grabbed Faith's arm in an iron-strong grip. "Faith."

She blinked and then warmth slid through her. "Yeah. That's me." Man, he was hot. All right. The coming out of a coma and saying her name was kind of cool. But it was time to get to the truth. "Who are you?"

He shook his head. *"Gde, chert voz'mi, ya?"*

She blinked. Wow. A Russian model? His eyes were a metallic aqua. Was he wearing contacts? "Okay, buddy. Enough with the joke." She gently tried to pull loose, but he held her in place, his hand large enough to encircle her entire bicep.

He blinked, his eyes somehow hardening. They started to glow an electric blue, sans the green. "Where am I?" His voice was low and gritty. Hoarse to a point that it rasped through the room, winding around them.

The colored contacts were seriously high-tech.

"You speak Russian and English. Extraordinary." She twisted her wrist toward her chest, breaking free. The guy was probably paid by the hour. "The jig is up, handsome." Whatever his rate, he'd earned every dime. "Tell Simons to come out from wherever she's hiding." Faith might have to clap for her best friend. This deserved applause.

The guy ripped the fake bandage off his head and then yanked the EKG wires away from his chest. He shoved himself to a seated position. The bed groaned in protest. "Where am I?" He partially turned his head to stare at the now-silent monitor. "What the hell is that?" His voice still sounded rough and sexy.

Just how far was he going to take this? "The joke is over." Faith glanced at Barclay on the floor, who was staring at the patient with wide eyes. "You're quite the actor, Dr. Barclay." She smiled.

Barclay grabbed a chair and hauled himself to his feet, the muscles in his forearms tightening. "Wh—what's happening?"

Faith snorted and moved past him, looking down the now-darkened hallway. Dim yellow emergency lights ignited along the ceiling. "They've cut the lights." Delight filled her. She lifted her voice. "Simons? Payback is a bitch, but this is amazing. Much better than April fool's." After Faith had filled Louise's car with balloons filled with sparkly confetti—guaranteed to blow if a door opened and changed the pressure in the vehicle—Simons had sworn vengeance.

"Louise?" Faith called again. Nothing. Just silence. Faith sighed. "You win. I bow to your pranking abilities."

Ice started to form on the wall across the doorway. "How are you doing that?" Faith murmured, truly impressed.

A growl came from behind her, and she jumped, turning back to the man on the bed.

He'd just *growled*?

She swallowed and studied him. What the heck? The saline bag appeared genuine. Moving quickly, she reached his arm. "They are actually pumping saline into your blood?" Okay. The joke had officially gone too far.

Something that looked like pain flashed in his eyes. "Who died? I felt their deaths, but who?"

She shook her head. "Come on. Enough." He was an excellent actor. She could almost feel his agony.

The man looked at her, his chin lowering. Sitting up on the bed, he was as tall as she was, even though she was standing in her favorite two-inch heeled boots. Heat poured off him, along with a tension she couldn't ignore.

She shivered again, and this time it wasn't from the cold.

Keeping her gaze, he tore out the IV.

Blood dribbled from his vein. She swallowed and fought the need to step back. "All right. Too far, Simons," she snapped. "*Waaaay* too far."

Barclay edged toward the door. "I don't understand what's happening."

Faith shook her head. "Occam's razor, Dr. Barclay." Either the laws of physics had just changed or this was a joke. The simplest explanation was that Simons had just won the jokester title for all time. "Enough of this, though. Who are you?" she asked the actor.

He slowly turned his head to study Dr. Barclay before focusing back on her. "When did the shield fall?"

The shield? He seemed so serious. Eerily so. Would Simons hire a crazy guy? No. Faith tapped her foot and heat rose to her face, her temper stirring. "Listen. This has been fantastic, but it's getting old. I'm done."

The guy grabbed her arm, his grip unbreakable this time. "Did both shields fail?"

Okay. Her heart started to beat faster. Awareness pricked along her skin. "Let go of me."

"No." The guy pushed from the bed and shrugged out of his gown, keeping hold of her. "What the fuck?" He looked at the Foley catheter inserted into his penis and then down to the long white anti-embolism stockings that were supposed to prevent blood clots.

Faith's breath caught. Holy shit. The catheter and TED hose were genuine. And his penis was huge. She looked up at his face. The TED hose might add a realistic detail to a joke, but no way would any responsible medical personnel insert a catheter for a gag. Simons wouldn't have done that. "What's happening?" Faith tried to yank her arm free, but he held her tight.

Dr. Barclay looked from her to the mostly naked male. "Who are you?" he whispered.

"My name is Ronan," the guy said, reaching for the catheter, which was attached to a urine-collection bag at the end of the bed. "What fresh torture is this?"

"Um," Faith started.

His nostrils flared. "Why would you collect my piss?"

Huh? "We're not," she protested. "You were in a coma. That's just a catheter."

He gripped the end of the tube, his gaze fierce.

"No—" Faith protested just as he pulled it out, grunting and then snarling in what had to be intense pain.

God. Was he on PCP or something? She frantically looked toward Barclay and mouthed the words *security* and *Get the nurse out of here*.

Barclay nodded and turned, running into the hallway.

"Where are we?" Ronan asked, drawing her toward him.

She put out a hand to protest, smashing her palm into his ripped abdomen. "Please. Let me go." She really didn't want to kick him in his already reddening penis. "You could've just damaged your urethra badly."

He started dragging her toward the door, his strength beyond superior. A sprawling tattoo covered his entire back. It looked like…a dark image of his ribs with lighter spaces between? Man, he was huge. "We must go."

Oh, there was no *we*. Whatever was happening right now wasn't good, and she had to get some space to figure this out. "I don't want to hurt you," she said, fighting his hold.

He snorted.

She drew in air and kicked him in the back of the leg, twisting her arm to gain freedom.

Faster than she could imagine, he pivoted, moving right into her. Heat and muscle and strength. He more than towered over her, fierce even though he was naked. She yelped and backpedaled, striking up for his nose.

He blocked her punch with his free hand and growled again, fangs sliding down from his incisors.

She stopped moving and her brain fuzzed. *Fangs?* Okay. This wasn't a joke. Somebody was seriously messing with her, and maybe they wanted her hurt. She couldn't explain the eyes and the fangs, so this had to be bad. This guy was obviously capable of inflicting some real damage. His eyes morphed again to the electric blue, and somehow he broadened even more, looking more animalistic than human.

"I don't understand," she said, her voice shaking as her mind tried to make sense of what her eyes were seeing. "Who are you? Why were you unconscious in a coma? How did you know my name?"

He breathed out, his broad chest moving with the effort. The fangs slowly slid back up, and his eyes returned to the sizzling aqua. "My name is Ronan Kayrs, and I was unconscious because the shield fell." He eyed her, tugging her even closer. "I know your name because I spent four hundred years seeing your face and feeling your soft touch in my dreams."

"My—my face?" she stuttered.

His jaw hardened even more. "And that was *before* I'd accepted my death."

On behalf of 1001 Dark Nights,

Liz Berry and M.J. Rose would like to thank ~

Steve Berry
Doug Scofield
Kim Guidroz
Jillian Stein
InkSlinger PR
Dan Slater
Asha Hossain
Chris Graham
Fedora Chen
Kasi Alexander
Jessica Johns
Dylan Stockton
Richard Blake
BookTrib After Dark
and Simon Lipskar

Made in the USA
Middletown, DE
22 March 2018